ENTICE

Dark Odyssey Club Fantasies Book 1

KHARDINE GRAY
FAITH SUMMERS

ENTICE

USA Today Bestselling Author
Khardine Gray
Writing As
Faith Summers

DARK ROMANCE NOTE

WARNING: This book is a standalone **DARK ROMANCE.** This book contains scenes that may be triggering to some readers and should be read by those only 18+ or older. **

AUTHOR NOTE

Please note: Faith Summers is the Dark Romance pen name of USA Today Bestselling Author Khardine Gray

Copyright © 2020 by Khardine Gray Please note: Faith Summers is the Dark Romance pen name of USA Today Bestselling Author Khardine Gray

All rights reserved.

Entice Copyright © 2020 by Khardine Gray

Cover design © 2019 by Book Cover Couture

No part of this book may be reproduced in any form or by any electronic or mechanical means, including information storage and retrieval systems, without written permission from the author, except for the use of brief quotations in a book review.

This work is copyrighted. Apart from any use as permitted under the Copyright Act 1968, no part may be reproduced, copied, scanned, stored in a retrieval system, recorded or transmitted, in any form or by any means, without the prior written permission of the author, except for the use of brief quotations in a book review.

This is a work of fiction. Names, characters, businesses, places, events and incidents are either the products of the author's imagination or used in a fictitious manner. Any resemblance to actual persons, living or dead, or actual events is purely coincidental.

The author asserts that all characters and situations depicted in this work of fiction are entirely imaginary and bear no relation to any real person.

No part of this book may be reproduced in any form or by any electronic or mechanical means, including information storage and retrieval systems, without written permission from the author, except for the use of brief quotations in a book review.

The following story contains mature themes, strong language, and sexual situations.

It is intended for mature readers. All characters are 18+ years of age, and all sexual acts are consensual.

WELCOME TO THE DARK ODYSSEY.

Welcome to The Dark Odyssey.
We hope you enjoy our masquerade parties.
Our aim is to connect you with your wildest fantasies.
To thrill and excite you all at once in a place where you can just be you.
When the masks go on and the lights go out, you decide what happens next.

CHAPTER ONE

GISELLE

Sexy, confident, daring...
That is what I will be tonight.
I'm going to be this sexy, confident woman and leave the me of the past behind.
Tonight, I will be wild and daring.
Not Miss Goodie-Two-shoes Giselle St. John, who spends her life buried in law books.
It's my birthday, and this is the new me. I look like a million dollars and feel like a new woman doing something different and unknown.
Tonight is about me, and I'm living it, especially with the big day that awaits me tomorrow as I start my new job as a junior associate at Tanners.
What is the point of being en route to a successful legal career if you have no life?
Or, if you're me, watching your ex-boyfriend inform the world how badly I sucked the life out of him, and he is enjoying his newfound happiness with his host of Victoria's Secret models

because he kicked his boring-as-shit ex-girlfriend, aka me, to the curb.

That is how Kirk described me on national TV days ago for all to hear.

Bastard.

I wish someone could have told me years ago to stay away from him. It would have saved me years of stress and the heartache of a bad breakup because yes, he did indeed kick me to the curb.

I do wish, though, he could see me tonight.

I may be nervous as hell dressed in a violet baby doll negligee under a matching silk robe and heels to match, but I'd gladly inform his ass I'm anything but boring *and* I don't drain the life out of people. I know how to have fun, and I can be wild.

That's why I'm here tonight, at The Dark Odyssey, a sex club.

I'm here with Rachel and Jia, my two best friends, who often frequent the place. We're third in the line to get our masks for the masquerade-themed lingerie parties they hold here every night. The two are dressed alike in blood red slips with sheer netted robes.

Rachel turns to me and giggles, tucking a lock of her dark hair behind her ear. Of the three of us, she's the wildest. I've known her since I was five, and I swear my first lesson on sex was taught by her. Over the years, she's kept up to date on everything, so this is the norm for her.

"Can you look a little less stiff?" she says to me and shakes her head.

Jia gives me a smile. "Yes, dear, it's not you who's supposed to be stiff. Save that for your guy."

They both start laughing.

Rachel leans into me and gives me a pointed stare. "You always get this stiff look on your face when you're thinking about Kirk. Tonight is about leaving all the shit outside."

She points at the doors a couple has just walked through. You can tell they're VIP because they walk on ahead past the line and carry on down the corridor, strolling along like they come here on the regular.

I return my attention to Rachel and nod. She's right. I'm leaving the shit outside. All of it.

"Believe me, I am," I say, looking from her to Jia. "There's no shit on my mind. I'm just nervous... but it's the excited kind."

I groan inwardly when they exchange disbelieving glances, confirming my suspicion since Rachel came up with the idea to come here. Pure and simple, she didn't expect me to say yes.

They're both excited for me to join them in the wildness they usually get up to, but they're expecting me to flake out, freak, then leave.

The shit with Kirk happened days ago, not only embarrassing me but crushing me because it felt like the last blow. When I declared I wanted to go wild for my birthday and bring in my twenty-sixth year doing something different, she didn't expect me to agree to a wild adventure at The Dark Odyssey.

I did, though, much to their shock, which is how we ended up here.

"Well, just know there's nothing to be nervous of," says Jia, the girl who's been coming here since she was eighteen even though you have to be twenty-one to get in. "It's fantasy and adventure."

"Yes, but if it gets too much... we'll understand if you leave," Rachel imparts with a crude accusatory look that's telling me she's thinking back to when I left her cousin's bachelorette party because there were too many strippers.

I felt it was disrespectful to Kirk to have some guy up in my face with his cock hanging out wanting to show me a good time.

They thought I was being too good. Turns out they were right. That was the first time I thought Kirk cheated on me, although I had no real proof.

"I'm not leaving," I tell them with a nod of my head and a lift in my shoulders that makes my long brown hair drift around my elbows.

"You sure?" Rachel quirks a brow.

"Yes," I answer with more insistence, and again they look at each other.

"Okay, Giselle... it'll be good if you stay. I think you'll find it different, and you may surprise yourself."

"I'll be fine." I smile because it's all I can do.

To be honest, I'm just thinking this is the wildest thing I've ever done, and I have no other thoughts past that. Except the fact that I'm still wound up about all the negative things Kirk said about me. As if it wasn't hard enough to move on from a three-year relationship and the fact that he's the only man I've ever been with. After being broken up for the last six months, his words were like salt on a reopened wound that had been healing.

We get to the head of the line, and the receptionist greets us. She's beautiful with bright auburn hair and large green eyes.

"Welcome to the Dark Odyssey, ladies," she beams. "Are you here by yourselves looking for an adventure, or are you meeting someone?"

"We're here for an adventure," Rachel answers for the three of us, and the receptionist smiles.

"Fantastic, here are your masks and bags," she says and hands us each a black mask and a little sheer bag that reminds me of the sort you'd get at a wedding with a party favor. It's smaller, though, with a silver coin inside.

She sees me looking at mine and smiles wider.

"The coin is to give to the person you want to spend the night with or have an adventure with."

"I would just give it to them?" I ask. I can't imagine it. What would I do? Just walk up to a guy and hand him the coin?

I'm going for this wild thing, but this borders more on bravery.

She nods, and Rachel and Jia giggle.

"It cuts out the worry of shyness. People know what the coin means, so if you meet someone and you gel, then you take it from there." She makes it sound so easy. Maybe it is.

"Thank you," I answer.

"Have fun." She laughs, and Rachel links her arm with mine, pulling me along.

"It will be great," Rachel muses as we hand over our jackets at the coat check.

We keep our mini purses holding our phones, put our masks on, and the three of us walk down the marble floor corridor leading down to a huge set of doors.

The doors open automatically for us, and we head inside, stepping straight onto the dance floor, enveloped by the vibrant club mix, the multicolor strobe lights, and the people dancing.

Just like a normal club, there are bouncers at the door. Hunky-looking guards who look like they were pulled from the set of a film.

Fascination is the first thing to take me because everyone is wearing masquerade masks of all types and description, and the majority of women are dressed in lingerie. It looks more like an erotic carnival, and the way the place is artfully decorated alone is enough to suck you in.

The beauty becomes more apparent as we walk further into the clash of bodies having a great time.

The multiple levels with baroque balconies attached to it are stunning. A bar, heaving with people, is ahead of us on the dance floor. Exotic dancers, some topless, are stationed on podiums on either side of the bar, and they too are dressed in lingerie with masks.

What takes my breath away, however, is the gold ceiling that seems endless. It all really does have a Venetian, European, feel to it. Many years ago, my dad took me to Venice, and I loved it. This feels like standing in one of the theaters.

I was about to continue the comparison, but before I can even bring my eyes down, I see the first thing to truly shock me.

There are naked acrobats on aerial hoops having sex. Like, actual sex, and in the air.

I have to squint and crane my neck because I'm not sure if what I'm seeing is real.

But it is, and it's not just one couple. The aerial hoop is

connected to some rotating device attached to the ceiling, and as that couple floats away into the darkness, another comes into view in a different sexual position where the guy has the woman hooked around his waist. The man's legs seem to be the only thing holding them up.

They float by, and my eyes move down only to freeze again at the scene before me.

It makes me stop mid track, and my lips part.

I don't know how I didn't see it before, but along the sidelines of the dance floor are cubicles and alcoves with padded leather sofas. Inside the cubicles are people having sex.

They seriously are... and just like that too, with everyone watching.

Of course, I knew I'd see people having sex. It's a sex club. I just didn't think it would be as... well, like *this*... not what I'm looking at.

Across from me is a woman with not just one but three guys. She's straddling guy number one while he pounds into her pussy, while guy number two pounds into her ass. Guy number three feeds her his cock. While the scene reminds me of something from a very wild porno, I can't look away.

I want to. I feel like I should, but I'm so intrigued and... aroused, that I can't.

I've heard things about The Dark Odyssey. I knew it was wild and unreal, but damn, this is sinfully wild.

Sinfully?

I don't know if simply describing the scene before me as sinful is enough.

A hand tugging on my elbow pulls me from my thoughts. It's Rachel. She looks at the scene too and smiles.

She leans in and says, "It's normal."

The music is loud, but I heard her, and I'm shocked. But I guess I would be if I'd only ever been with one guy and was of the part of the population who thinks sex is reserved for the bedroom.

"Come on," she says, pulling me away from the scene as the music changes to something more upbeat.

The crowd goes wild and again, and I'm immersed in the electric vibe of the place.

We start dancing, and I actually lose myself in the music. I'm so lost that I don't feel the weight of eyes on me until the song nearly ends.

It may be crazy to think someone could watch me in a crowd like this, but the intensity of the gaze is so strong that I turn around and find myself looking up at a man on the first-floor balcony who's definitely watching me.

Our eyes lock, and he makes a point of scanning my body. As he does, heat curls through me.

Although he's wearing a black mask that covers half his face, I can see he's gorgeous. His presence oozes wild sexual confidence, and the black button-down shirt he's wearing does a good job of showing off his wide, powerful, muscular shoulders. I can just make out a pair of black slacks too. The balcony covers the rest of him.

He has longish hair with the sides tapered, and although he's definitely a good thirty feet away from me, I can see the sharp structure of his exposed cheekbone and a light of interest in his eyes directed at me.

Aware that I'm staring, I turn away, back to Rachel, who's noticed I was looking at him.

Again, she leans in. "Confident, sexy, and daring. Remember?" She giggles, reminding me of my mantra of affirmation, and twirls around.

I laugh when a guy slips his arm around her and the two start dancing. To my left is Jia, and she too has found a guy.

None of this surprises me because this is something that always happens whenever we go out. No matter where we are. These two are the female versions of playboys. They like to play hard and believe life is for living it up.

I continue dancing but soon become lost; I don't even get to be the fifth wheel. Things seem to happen faster here.

When a guy with a gold mask starts dancing with me, that sensation of being watched returns.

The guy seems handsome enough from what I can see outside of his mask to catch my interest, but I lose him when I look over my shoulder, back to where I was previously staring. My mystery guy isn't where he was before. I can't see him anywhere, but I can feel him watching me.

It's so strange, or maybe it's me who feels strange.

The music changes again to something sensual and slow. Since I'm not paired up with anyone, I head to the bar.

A cute bartender with blond dreadlocks gives me a smile when I approach.

"Hi," I say.

"Wow," he replies, scanning my face. I guess I should be happy he's looking at my face and not my breasts, which I'm showing more of than usual. "What can I get you?"

"Just some water, please." I know that's not sexy, confident, or daring, but I'm a lightweight, and the last thing I want to do is get drunk at a place like this where I'm completely out of my element.

"*Water?*" He raises his brows. "Can't I at least get you some fruit punch? If I mix the fruit, it will make me look more creative. I'll feel like I'm doing something."

I chuckle. "Okay, I'll have fruit punch."

He tips his head and sets off to make my drink.

I watch him make the drink like he would a cocktail. He places it in a glass with fruit on the side, sugar syrup drizzled around the edge, and a little umbrella.

"That's on the house," he says as he places it before me.

"Thanks so much."

"Holler if you need anything else."

"I will."

He winks at me and moves to the next customer.

I sip on my drink and look to my left just in time to see a naked couple step into a glass box on the stage ahead of me. My eyes widen as I realize it's an exhibitionist box.

The couple look so excited. As they close the door on the box, it lifts into the air for everyone to see. The guy stands behind the woman and instantly starts to fuck her. I watch as their moves turn faster and faster until he has her pressed right against the glass. The look on her face is so... well, it's what I would call rapturous. It's not just happy, excited, or thrilled. It's more than elated.

The cheers of the crowd below that's gathered encourages them, and that's when I get it.

It's all for show. All of it. It's all a show to bring forward the fantasy. The people doing it do it, and the people watching can be intrigued too.

What's my fantasy?

I actually don't know.

"You look like you would enjoy that," says a voice behind me.

It pulls me away from the sight of the couple in the box the same way the intensity of the stare did when I was dancing.

I'm actually not surprised to see the voice and the stare belong to the same person. The same man.

What throws me is his presence. He's tall and towers over me at what I'd say is probably six feet six. I'm five four. In my heels, I barely reach the top of his chest.

He looked gorgeous standing on the balcony. Up close he's more. The exposed side of his face shows off a high cheekbone chiseled to perfection, and I wish I could see the other side of his face.

Especially as his bright blue eye takes me in with that interest that makes my body come alive.

I swallow hard, aware that I'm staring again, and I haven't answered his question.

His question-slash-statement of basically the exhibitionist box being my thing.

"I'm sorry, what?" I ask. This here is my chance to be confident, sexy, and daring. I'm here under the persona of such. Now I just have to work it.

The corner of his mouth slides into a sensual smile, and he leans closer.

"The exhibitionist box looks like your kind of thing. Ever been in there?" he asks. His smooth baritone voice is low in timbre, sexy just like him.

I'm flattered that he thinks I'm daring enough to have sex in public like that. Not boring or life sucking.

"No, I haven't."

"Oh." His gaze drops from my eyes, touches my lips, then flicks down to my cleavage and over my body for a once-over. "So, that's your fantasy?" He smiles wider.

My lips part, and I think about it. I imagine being taken in the exhibitionist box for all to see and somehow, I don't think of the part where people are watching. I remember the rawness of the couple and the way they looked. That's the part that entices me.

"I don't know," I answer, unable to keep the quiver out of my voice. "It seems... bold."

He chuckles deep and low. "I didn't think bold would be a problem for someone as sexy as you."

He thinks I'm sexy. I'm definitely liking this guy a lot.

"Well, there are just a lot of people watching."

"But the box fascinates you?"

I smile. "Maybe." I don't know what I'm saying. I guess I am probably being a bit too honest because the box did fascinate me. Something bold comes over me, though, the longer I stare at him. "Does the box fascinate you?"

"Yes," he answers without a moment's hesitation, and I can't help the image that sweeps through my mind of us inside the box, naked, of him taking me in that raw animalistic way I saw in the man as he owned the woman's body.

My mystery man smiles at me like he can tell what I'm thinking, and my cheeks flush.

"Is... that your fantasy?" I ask, homing in on the confidence I'm striving for.

"I don't know. Not sure what sort of fantasy I'll be living out tonight. I'm... still trying to find out. There's a lot to do here."

"Is there?" I looked at the website, but honestly, I was so focused on the part of just coming here that I didn't pay much attention to everything else. I know the place is huge with themed rooms and a sex dungeon. The owners really went to town in their creation of the fantasies.

"Yeah." His eyes sparkle like he just got an idea. "What's your name, sweetheart?"

The way he said that tempts me to tell him to just call me that, or whatever he wants.

"Giselle. My name's Giselle."

"Wow." He's the second man to say that to me tonight. When he says it, though, it effects my body more deeply. "Nice name. My name's Josh."

That suits him. I imagined him with a strong name like that.

"I like your name too."

"Thank you, Giselle. You're here with your friends?"

I raise my shoulders into a little shrug. "We're here for my birthday, though it looks like they've kind of deserted me."

A glint touches his eye. "Oh... happiest birthday to you."

"Thank you."

"I was about to explore. Do you want to come with me? Maybe you'll find the fantasy you're looking for."

Oh my God... if I go with him, I know what that means. Exploring a sex club with a gorgeous man looking at me the way he is can only lead to one thing.

And didn't I think that was going to possibly, *potentially*, happen by coming here?

Confident and sexy... daring...

The words run through my mind, and the molten heat in his eyes makes my answer come easier.

"Okay," I agree.

He holds out his hand to take mine, and I take it.

CHAPTER TWO

GISELLE

As we move away from the bar, I'm aware of his large hand covering mine and the way our fingers entwine.

The daring voice that's been whispering to me since I decided I was coming here tells me it's a sign of how my night will end.

He leads me to the first floor, where I'd first seen him, and stops by a large room that's as big as a hall, where all I can see is bodies clashing together. Naked bodies of the people in there having an orgy.

Until tonight I'd only ever heard of things like this and seen a hint of on TV a few times.

This is the real deal, and the sight is too much. I can't tell where the bodies begin or end.

All I see is arms and legs, and people moaning and groaning in a chorus of pleasure. There are men with women, women with women, men with men. It's every kind of pairing imaginable, everyone linked together.

A warm finger slides over the small of my back. I didn't even realize I was no longer holding Josh's hand. He's leaned down close to my ear. I turn to face him, and my cheek brushes against his.

"This your thing, sweetheart? You seem to like this too. We can go in... if you want."

My mouth goes dry, and I swallow past the lump that's formed in my throat.

"Or... is it too much?" he adds. "Too many hands everywhere. I don't know if I like the idea of sharing you... with *anyone*."

I can't process. Between him, his words, and the orgy in front of me, I'm lost in my thoughts.

"I'm... I... I think I'd like to look around more," I answer, and instead of taking my hand again, he keeps his hand on my back and ushers me away from the room and we walk down a dimly lit corridor.

"Orgy not your thing?" he asks with a wicked smile.

"I don't think so. It's too much." Too much for me, but he sounds like he would do it, or is well versed in it.

"I figured. It's your first time here, isn't it?" he observes, glancing at me as we walk.

"Yeah, do I stick out like a sore thumb?" I laugh nervously.

"No, I'm just perceptive. I watch people's reactions and try to figure out their inner thoughts. Just like I knew the orgy might be too much for you, but you'd be a natural in the exhibitionist box."

We stop, and he faces me, taking a lock of my hair.

"You think so?" I ask.

"I do think so, but you wouldn't be going inside so people can watch you. You'd be going in for the freedom of it. The wildness of the idea. The same way you'd fly the aerial hoops if you could."

I narrow my eyes at him. "You saw me when I came in?"

"I watch, and I see what I want to see." He watches the lock of hair curl around his finger and allows it to drift back to me. "Come, maybe you'll like this next attraction." He points, and we continue walking down the corridor.

"Attraction?"

"That's what the club owners call it. They think of everything as a show or an attraction to enhance the fantasy of the place, or create one."

I was right, then.

"Where are we going?" I ask when I hear water ahead of us. Water and more moans and groans.

"It's called The Halls of Fantasium." He looks ahead. The lights darken, and the music cuts.

It's all water, and as we turn, I see why it's called that. It looks like an erotic version of Fantasia.

We walk into a room that's filled with blue and lilac fluorescent lights. Mirrors shimmer, and the walls have sparkling water running down them like a waterfall.

Pressed against the walls are couples having sex.

This setting in here feels more intimate. Wild though it is because the couples are still having sex in the open, the way they touch each other is more sensual. I could imagine coming here with someone I'm in an actual relationship with. We'd do this for fun.

"You really like this," Josh states, and I look up at him, blushing.

"It's more subtle." I always avoid giving a definitive yes or no if I'm not too sure about something. It's a habit that's been drilled into me from being an attorney. Being neutral is safest.

He grins and takes my hand again. "Let's go this way if you like subtle."

We make our way into a room as dimly lit as the corridor was, but it's slightly darker.

I look around and realize it's just us. We take another step, and the floor looks like it moves, but it doesn't, really. It's water beneath a glass floor that flows and lights up a soft iridescent color as we walk on it.

"Oh wow," I muse.

"They have a thing about water here."

"What is it about water?"

"It's a natural aphrodisiac. *Subtle*."

"Oh..."

He releases my hand and walks around me, looking me up and down. I like what they've done in here; a sexual feeling is humming in the air, and the lighting isn't like most of those places where you'd turn the same color as the lights.

It makes it so I can still enjoy the man who's giving me so much attention.

"What are you doing?" I ask when he stops behind me and his eyes are glued to my ass. It's obvious he's checking me out, but I want to hear what's on his mind.

"Watching," he answers.

"Me?"

"Yes. I'm watching and wondering what your fantasy is."

"What about yours? What's your fantasy?" I turn to face him.

"Right now... it's you," he says, and desire pools low between my thighs.

"*Me?*" I ask, my voice barely above a whisper.

"It's you, and I'm wondering what you'd look like with the robe gone."

I don't think I've ever met anyone more forward than him, and I've certainly never met a man who looked at me the way he does. Like he wants to possess me.

Possess...

Own.

I don't know if that makes sense. It's the feeling I get, though, from his pensive stare, along with the feeling that he's being gentle with me. Feeding me spoonfuls of what he's truly like. It's the tone in his voice. Like he's holding back.

Since I never really intended on keeping the robe on, I take it off, and the coolness of the room graces my shoulders.

He stops just in front of me and takes me in. Like every man I've ever met, his eyes go straight to my breasts. You tend to get a lot of attention with double Ds. Double Ds in a baby doll negligee that makes my cleavage even deeper is practically the same thing as having a sign on me saying 'Please look'.

When he looks, though, I don't mind it.

He smiles, and his perfect white teeth sparkle against the light. "Well... now I'm wondering what you look like without the mask."

I remember reading this part on the website. You take off the mask when you want to reveal yourself, most often to the person you choose to be with for the night.

Since it's definitely not the first time he's been here, I'm sure he knows that.

"Do I get to see you, Giselle?"

"What would it mean?"

"What would you want it to mean?" he throws back.

At first, I smile, then I try to bite it back. "I don't know." That answer is me entirely. My fail-safe, and maybe the coward's way out. "What if I wanted to see you without your mask?"

"I have no problem with that, Giselle," he answers. "What if I wanted to give you my coin? Would you take it?" He walks around me again, and my heart stops. I swear it does.

This is it, the moment of choice, and I guess the moment I've been gearing up for since I stepped through the doors of The Dark Odyssey.

Sex, and sex with someone who isn't Kirk.

It's laughable that I would even think about it like that because it wasn't even like Kirk was really mine towards the end of our relationship. It all started when he got drafted to play pro ball for the Warriors, Chicago's home football team. He changed. That was a year before we ended, so I don't know why I'm even thinking about him now as Josh circles me, waiting for my answer. People might think the sun shines from Kirk's ass because as the quarterback, he led his team to victory at nationals, but he's got nothing on this guy.

Josh stops in front of me, waiting for my answer.

"I'd take it," I say, and something dark and sinful lights up his eyes.

CHAPTER THREE

GISELLE

His silver coin is in his pocket.

He pulls it out and shows it to me, then hands it to me.

Just like I took his hand earlier, I take the coin and look at it.

"Do... I have to give you mine?" I ask. I'm not sure if that's how it works. It would make sense to.

"How about you decide in a little while?" He lifts his chin, appraising me.

"A little while?"

"Yes... you might decide you've had enough fun with me and move on to someone else."

I'm not like that, but he doesn't know that. "What if you decided you wanted to move on to someone else?" I counter.

He moves closer, and my nerves scatter. "Call me old-fashioned, or maybe I have my own spin on the term, but if I give you my coin, it's you I want for the night, but you have a choice. You get to decide after the taster session."

My mouth waters.

"Taster session?" I ask, feeling like his echo now.

Another step closer, and my breath hitches. He's so close I

can smell the musky scent of his aftershave. It tickles my nose and makes my pussy clench with anticipation.

"I'm a firm believer in sampling and getting a taste of the main. How else will you know if you like what I have to offer?"

I can't bite back the smile that arches my lips. "I won't."

"So, how does a taster session sound, Giselle?"

"Good..." I answer. It's clear my body took over long ago, succumbing to curiosity.

"Well, maybe then I'll be deserving of your coin." That flash of something sinful returns to his eyes. It's predatory and dominating. It suits the strength in his personality. "I will need your permission to give you the taster. It might not be what you're used to for a first meeting, but then again, we did meet in a sex club." He holds my gaze, and my lungs constrict. "Do I have your permission, Giselle?"

"Yes," I say, as if by default. I don't think my body would allow any other answer than yes.

"Okay." He raises his hand to his mask and takes it off, smoothing it over his face, then his hair, and wow... the full vision of him takes my breath away.

I get the feeling he knew that would happen though.

In the subtle light, his blue eyes are more striking, and I see I was right about the deep angles and planes carved into his face.

He has a face that looks like God took his time to carve to perfection. He arches one dark brow, and the smile now reveals a dimple in his left cheek.

"Does my appearance please you?"

I don't know what kind of question that is. Maybe he just wants to hear me say yes.

"It does," I answer. I guess it's my turn now, so I pull the mask off my face and give my hair a shake when it gets tangled in it.

Thank God I seem to please him too.

"And me?" I ask. My voice sounds meeker than I want it to.

"You had me at hello," he replies, and I find I can't look away.

He steps even closer and lowers his mouth to my lips. I lift my chin, readying myself for his kiss. I don't know what I expected to feel when his lips touched mine, but it wasn't the rush of heat that pulses through my whole body. It makes me ache all over.

Fire sweeps through me, like someone poured liquid fire all over me, bathing me in it.

When he kisses me harder, a little moan escapes my lips. He takes advantage of that moment to sweep his tongue over mine, and damn...

I melt against him. I melt, and I press into the hard walls of his chest while he cups my face and slides his hand into my hair to deepen the kiss.

The kiss makes me hotter, then it turns from hot to hungry, to greed, and he moves with me over to the wall. It pulls my attention away from the thrill of him when it lights up the same iridescent color as the floor.

He moves away from my lips, and we both look at the glass wall and the water flowing behind. It's like being immersed in a sea of fluorescent water.

I'm looking at it, and he's looking at me, eyes scanning me with the hunger and greed that resonated from the kiss.

Up close to the light, his eyes become brighter with the color, and sexier.

"More?" he asks, lingering on the sound. It has the desired effect on me because I feel the tug deep inside my body that is definitely begging for more.

"More."

On my word he moves to my neck, pushing me into the wall as he presses a firm palm to the flat of my stomach.

He places hot kisses all along my neck, and I suck in a sharp breath when his fingers run over the already diamond-hard points of my nipples.

He fills his palms with my breasts and starts squeezing and massaging, then he slides the silk of my negligee away from my left breast, then the right, allowing the straps to glide down my shoulders.

He looks at my breasts, focusing on them, and I wonder if he's trying to commit me to memory.

It's only then that the thought hits me once more that he's the second man to see me like this. I push that awareness away because I don't want to think of Kirk right now. I want the newness of this experience and all it will bring.

Josh takes care of all my worries and anything that was about to enter my mind by lowering his lips to my left nipple to close them over the tip. He sucks and, holy hell, it feels so damn good.

He sucks like he's tasting me, sampling me, and I can admit now that if all we did was this all night, I'd be happy with what I got.

He alternates from one breast to the other, giving each the same attention, and that's when I feel the tug of a greedy orgasm pulling deep in my pussy.

I'm torn between emotions clashing inside me, the build of pleasure that takes me higher as he sucks, and the almost tortuous feeling that gnaws away at my insides. That's a result of my body being starved of attention for far too long.

I slide my hands through Josh's hair, encouraging him to continue his feast on me, and he does.

He sucks harder, and fucking hell, I lose control, and my mind slips away. I'm lost in raw pleasure when his hands slide up my thigh and over the silk of my panties. He pushes a finger into my pussy, and a groan rumbles in my chest.

The sound turns me on so much it pushes the build of pleasure even higher. Pleasure fueled by the fire of the wildness in his touch.

"Fuck, you're so wet," he mutters, taking a break from the wild suckle on my breasts so he can lift the hem of my negligee and get a good look at his fingers working me.

I answer him with a moan. I can't talk. He slides another finger inside me and plants his free hand next to me, lowering his face to mine so we're at eye level.

"Does this feel good, Giselle? I wouldn't want to be doing anything in the taster that didn't make you say yes to the main course." His warm breath tickles my nose.

"Yesssss... It feels good," I stutter and rest my hands on the width of his shoulders to keep myself from falling over as he speeds up.

"Does that mean you want more?" he beckons in a menacing voice.

Fuck, I arch my back away from the wall and press into him.

"Do you want more, Giselle, or... should I stop?"

Stop?

Fuck no. No way in hell am I letting him stop doing what he's doing to me.

"More, Josh... I want more," I cry out, happy that we're the only ones in here, and close my eyes, squeezing them shut.

He shocks me, however, by stopping. It forces my eyes open, and I wonder if I did or said something wrong.

He holds my gaze and catches my face with one hand, sliding his fingers down to my neck. The hold is almost threatening for the slight tension in his grip, but his eyes say something else. His eyes and the fact that his fingers are still deep in my pussy.

"Say my name again," he commands. I realize then it was the first time I've said his name. He's called me by name many times, but I've only said his name just once.

"Josh," I breathe, and he smiles in that predatory manner that now has a feral vibe to it.

"I could get used to that, Giselle. Tempting a man like me isn't always a good thing. We find it hard to resist, so break me gently if you don't like what you see or feel."

Like most things tonight, I think I might be right in thinking this guy can't be broken.

He doesn't need gentle; he has no use for it. That is just for my benefit.

"I like what I see, and what I feel," I assure him. I can't believe myself, and I'm pretty sure my friends wouldn't believe this was me either. Me getting ready to have sex with a stranger, a man I just met.

He pushes me back against the wall and starts sliding his fingers in and out of me again.

"Spread your legs wider for me, sweetheart."

Sweetheart...

Something triggers inside me every time he's said that. Something that makes me yield to his every command.

I spread my legs wide, and he starts pumping harder and faster, finger-fucking me so hard I see stars.

A deep chuckle rumbles in his chest. "You like that a lot." It's a statement of fact.

I nod, and he releases my neck so he can crouch down.

I swallow as he looks up at me and pulls his fingers out to lick off the glistening juice. I catch my breath, but the next second sees me losing it all over again as he nuzzles his face between my thighs, spreading them wider so he can have better access to my pussy, and oh God, as he presses his tongue into me, I grab his shoulders again.

That's it. I can't take any more. I thrash against him and groan. I'm at the peak of pleasure now, and I can no longer control myself.

A sharp gasp falls from my lips as his clever tongue lashes over the swollen bud of my clit, making the sensation build that much more. It drives me wilder, and I writhe against his face.

His tongue is as ruthless as his touch, raw and unforgiving. Yet everything is aimed at giving me pleasure. I want it. I crave it.

One more circle over my pleading bud sends overlapping waves of fire over me, and my head falls back. I cry out into the release that takes me.

He grabs my ass and holds me to his face so he can drink. The licking now becomes exactly that, *drinking.* He drinks and laps up everything until there's nothing left.

The door opens, and a couple walks in. They look at us like this, and I don't even think to cover myself or hide. I don't want to do anything to ruin this, or break the feeling. So, I stay there just the way I am, doing exactly what my body wants me to do.

I'm practically doubled over Josh with my breasts hanging out for all to see while he drinks my release from my pussy. I'm still moaning and groaning, no different to the people I've witnessed tonight who've become passion's slaves.

The couple continues on through the next door, and Josh and I are alone again.

He releases me and stands but catches me when I stumble.

His hair is slightly ruffled from my fingers in it, but it just makes him look sexier.

"That was the taster, sweetheart... do you want more, Giselle?"

Confident, sexy, and daring has definitely been good to me tonight. I want it all, everything.

I reach for the little pouch I have clipped to the side of my negligee and take out my silver coin. He takes it when I hand it to him, his smile firm and set. He knows he has me where he wants me. Exactly where he wants me.

He flips the coin and places it in his back pocket. I place his in the pouch. I want to keep it, to remember tonight. It's one night, and I won't see him again, unless I come back here, and who's to say that he'll want me like this again?

He takes the pouch from me and sets it on the floor, right by my feet. His gaze flicks up to meet mine, and a smile is in his eyes as he runs his fingers up my legs and up to my panties. I allow him to take them off, and I allow him to take off the negligee, leaving me naked. Everything gone but the heels.

"Those stay," he says, his eyes roaming the length of my body.

Being bold, I take charge and step closer to him, tugging on the edge of his shirt.

"You, I want these off too," I tell him in a playful voice that sounds foreign to me.

He bends down to kiss me, and I kiss him back, but he tugs on my bottom lip in a truly sexy way that makes me wet all over again for him.

Stepping back, he reaches for his shirt and undoes the top buttons, allowing him to lift the rest of it over his head.

I have to swallow again to stop myself from drooling when I see the masterpiece of a body he uncovers. Muscles on muscles greet me, inked with black tattoos artistically decorating the width of his chest.

All Japanese characters. There are a lot, and I can't see some of the smaller ones on the edge of his hip. What I can see is enough to class his body as the one I want to always remember.

His lips arch, and a wild smile dances across his mouth as he pulls a condom from his back pocket.

"I can use this, but I'm clean. You?"

The thought of having him inside me with no barriers sends a spiral of ecstasy through me.

"I'm clean, and on the pill," I answer.

The condom pack floats to the floor, joining his shirt, and he undoes his belt buckle. It clinks as it falls away and he unzips his fly, allowing his pants to drift down his legs.

The massive bulge of his cock pressing against his boxers fascinates me and arouses me at the same time. He pushes his boxers down his legs, and his cock springs free. It's as massive as it looked pressed against the front of his boxers. Satisfaction washes over his face when he sees the way I look at him, and he finishes taking off his clothes.

With a growl, he reaches for me and turns me to face the wall. Looking at the glass wall glow as I touch it and the water flow beneath my fingers adds to the thrill.

I glance over my shoulder when he grabs my hips, lines his cock up against my pussy lips, and plunges in.

That makes me gasp and snap my gaze back around to face the wall.

Holy hell, I didn't think it would feel so good. I'm wet, but he's big, and I'm so tight he fills me up completely.

"Fucking hell, Giselle, your pretty pussy is so tight," he groans and starts pumping into me.

His cock pulses inside me as he pulls out a little, and I cry out when he drives back in and starts fucking me. He fucks me hard, pounding into me so hard my breasts bounce painfully against my chest and my hair falls forward over my face.

Lifting my hips, I take him pound after pound as he owns my body, his cock searing into me with delicious heat. The scalding heat devours me, and I'm left at his mercy. My mind isn't present anymore, and just when I'm about to go over the edge, he stops. He just stops like earlier when he was fingering me.

He pulls out again and turns me around to face him. When he picks me up, I wrap my legs around him so my heels can dig into his back.

"Perfect," he groans, settling me back down onto his cock.

The instant he does, the exhilaration of the skin-to-skin contact takes me, and he takes me too.

I'm there again, at the brink of orgasm.

"Josh, I'm coming," I cry.

"That's okay, baby, let me fuck you until you come."

I hold on tight to his shoulders as he fucks me. His pumps speed up, and I cling to him as he practically impales me with his cock. He fucks me harder, and we both cry out.

I throw my head back, arching my back, but he catches my head and pulls me back to his lips to kiss me.

He kisses me as we both come. The spray of his hot cum floods my passage, making it quake, and my release mingles with his.

We're still kissing even as I climb down from the high and the luxuriating sensation of being his.

Josh pulls away from my lips, but he's still holding me.

He studies me, and I see it in his eyes. The same thing I feel. I see it.

The need for more.

"Spend the night with me, Giselle," he requests, and I nod.

"Yes."

CHAPTER FOUR

JOSH

I'm always thrown when I get back to the real world.

This time, though... damn.

I don't think I've ever experienced anything like her.

Giselle....

She was the last thing I saw when I closed my eyes as sleep came for me.

I can never beat sleep when it does that.

I can go for a max of two days without sleeping before I crash. Last night, it practically came for me and swallowed me whole after I devoured the beautiful brunette.

As a VIP guest of The Dark Odyssey and a close friend to Gabe Giordano, one of the club owners, I get certain privileges.

Call it the VIP treatment with access to one of the suites reserved for special guests. Gabe and the other owners have private suites, but they set the place up so there are a few other suites guests like me can book, or use at short notice, like last night.

That's how Giselle and I ended up exploring each other's

bodies in every which way all night. I think I tried out every sexual position I could conjure up on her.

Foolishly, when I woke, I imagined waking up with her in my arms.

But she'd left.

She'd left, as expected, and reality of the distraction she'd been came rushing back to me. All I have left is her coin.

I rub it between my fingers as I sit back in my office chair, listening to my father talk to me like I'm a child.

I'm pretending to listen and trying not to show just how mad I am at him for the shit he's decided to dish me, all because he doesn't approve of the way I live my life.

"Joshua, are you listening to me?" he says, staring at me hard. He was pacing around while delivering his speech. The man didn't even allow me to get coffee before he barged into my office to start the daily sermon.

Rule number one: I'm not to sleep with the new associate.

Rule number two: I'm to hire a decent secretary and stop fucking the temps.

Okay...He didn't say *'fucking'*. Dad never swears. I'm sure he thinks God would strike him with lightening if he did.

I stare at him, my face brazen and deadpan, like I used to when I was a child.

If that is how he wishes to treat me, then fine.

I'll be the first to admit that I have a colorful past, and yes, I did and have been known to sleep around the office, more so in my younger days. But he's failed to notice that I've changed a lot and taken my work more seriously because I want the responsibility of running the new branch of Tanners.

I know when to be serious and when to play, and I don't play or fuck around at work anymore. That was the change I made to my life two years ago when the opportunity for this job first came about.

What's got me in this shit is him hearing that I slept with one of the temps, and he started to freak. She doesn't even work here anymore. He thinks this will be history repeating itself from five years ago when I got involved with Marsha, a budding associate.

She got pissed at me when it was clear we were just screwing around, and when she left, she took a host of high value clients with her because she was one of the senator's daughters. Dad has been mad at me ever since. Everything I do now is under scrutiny.

Now there's this shit. Unfair shit that shouldn't count. He's making me compete for the job. Pitting me against Riley, my cousin. A guy I loathe.

Riley and I are both senior partners here, but we are always at war.

"Joshua." He says my name with more insistence. My parents are the only people who full-name me. Everyone else calls me Josh.

"Dad... I'm still pissed as fucking shit at you," I answer and smile at his reaction. He hates me swearing.

My parents had me later in life. I'm thirty years old. Although he doesn't look it, Dad is seventy-one. Mom just turned seventy.

They're what you call old school, and they had a strict upbringing. My grandfather on Dad's side was a lieutenant in the army and fought in the Second World War. Mom's dad was a Baptist minister, and I'm pretty sure she blames me for the heart attack that took him a few years back when my asshole of a cousin told him I practically live in the sex club.

"Joshua, you think this is funny?" Dad says, nostrils flared. "Do you want the job or not?"

"Dad... I can't even with you today. How can you stand there and ask me that?" This whole conversation is the thing that caused me to lose sleep.

Work is the thing that usually makes me lose sleep because I'm the only attorney at the firm who takes on the difficult cases. I'm the only attorney here who can win a twisted-as-shit intellectual property dispute, coming out on top every single time, but despite that, I have to compete for a job I've been working so hard for. A job I thought was mine, hands down.

His shoulders slump. "Joshua, this is a multi-billion-dollar firm. It's simple. That is what it is, and I can't run around after you, cleaning up the mess you make with a project as big as this. Here I can keep tabs on you, and I have a handle on things. If I give you control over the new building, I need to trust that you can be the face of the firm. I need to trust that you will be the man I want you to be."

I seethe. "I'm not that now? Despite everything I've done, I'm not that guy yet? But fucking Riley is?" That motherfucker has had it in for me since birth.

Fucking asshole... he's always been in competition with me. What rubs me the wrong way is, I know deep down that my parents wish I could be more like him. The Goody-Two-shoes prick who does everything perfectly.

"Joshua, Riley is a good option to lead the firm. If this were down to a question on expertise alone, you'd win hands down, but it's not. It's a lot more than a question of who's better than whom. This is the way it will work, and it starts today with the new associate. Since I have to focus on the new training program, I need you to take over her training. The training I was going to give her. Three months with her and getting this department in order. That's what I want from you. And you need a secretary. No more temps. Most of all, I need you to shape up."

As if I haven't been shaping up. I keep my silence because he'll start talking about women and shit again. What he wants is for me to get married. That's the topic he's drifting toward. He's been finding ways to mention that a lot lately.

A small smile inches over his mouth. "Joshua, Jennifer isn't as bad as you think. She's a good woman," he says with a determined nod, and I try not to roll my eyes at him.

I bite down hard on my back teeth. Now's not the time for me to give an answer to that. Jennifer is Corrine's daughter. Mom's best friend. So, they met at church.

I won't tell Dad that Jennifer was the reason the Petersons

got divorced because Mrs. Peterson caught her riding her husband's eighty-year-old cock. And I won't tell Dad it was Jennifer's fault why Officer Beaumont's wife-to-be left him at the altar.

Cheating. The woman is a cheat who loves money and cock that doesn't belong to her. But I won't tell Dad that because he still remembers the sweet little girl he accompanied to her first communion. He thinks of her as heaven sent and literally like God loaned the world one of his angels.

I won't tell him either that while I might be unattached and look like a suitable candidate to the ethereal being he thinks she is, she'd only have me because of my wealth.

I may be a bastard who thinks he owns the world and has women at his beck and call eating out of his hands more often than not because of my wealth, and my looks, but there's a part of me who wouldn't want to be married to a woman who wants to be with me just for that.

I'm too possessive to tolerate cheating, and I don't share things that belong to me. Since I expect that, I would be the same. That is how it would be.

But... I'll humor him.

Three months. I can look like I'm trying to play by his rules for three months, get control of the new firm, and then do whatever the fuck I want.

I have my own stipulations, however.

"I'm telling you it's a straight up no to Jennifer," I inform him. "I want to control the new firm, but I will not have you hang a woman over my head hoping I'll marry her. I'm not doing it."

He frowns, and I know then he really was hoping to squeeze that in.

"Joshua—"

I hold up my hand. "No, Dad, it's wrong. Even you know that. I'll see the new associate through her training, and I'll whip the department in shape. That's work related. You can't rule my personal life."

"Joshua, you are the face of the company as my son. Inside and outside of work. It doesn't matter where you are. People who know you as a Tanner will automatically think of the firm. I wish you could live your life a little more civilized. You are always at the sex club, and the way you live is just.... *unsavory.* Take it down a notch."

Anger fills him again, and he's about to go off into another lecture when a knock sounds at the door.

This is supposed to be the associate now. It's nine. She's right on time, so I can give her credit for that.

I hate associates. I hate anybody training under me because mostly they don't get me. And... I hate brainiacs, most especially the Stanford ones who think they know it all. I went to Georgetown, and I can wipe the floor with anybody from anywhere.

He sprang this woman on me, and I was hoping to get rid of her. I didn't even bother to read her file when Dad told me she went to Stanford.

Dad looks to me and points. I hate anybody, whoever they are, pointing at me.

"Remember what I said. You will not sleep with her..." he warns, and I smile.

"Come in," I say instead of answering him.

The door pushes open, and for the first time in weeks, I really believe God has turned his sight back to me.

I'm frozen in time, space, and everything, the same way I was last night when I saw her enter the club.

At my door stands a very wide-eyed Giselle.

Wide-eyed and beautiful with that luscious, long brown hair, coffee-colored eyes, and a body that was made for serious sinning.

Her cheeks turn crimson with a blush that flushes to her neck when she sees me.

I should be shocked by the coincidence, but instead, that animalistic part of me that wanted to take her and make her mine last night comes out.

She's my associate.

Looks like the day just got heaps better.

CHAPTER FIVE

JOSH

I try to stop grinning.

I must look psychotic with the smile that's spread across my face.

Dad smile's too at the beauty, beckoning her to come in.

I could kick myself now for not reading the file. If I had, I would have gotten her name days ago. Last night, I would have at least picked up on some element of coincidence of meeting two Giselles in one week. We might have had some conversation that would allude to the fact that she's the same person I've referred to as 'that woman I'm training' for the last three days.

"Joshua, this is Giselle St. John," Dad says, and I rise to my feet, holding out my right hand for her to shake. In my left is the coin. *Her coin.* I wonder what she did with mine.

"Hello," I say, shaking her dainty hand as she gives it to me. It feels the same as last night. Like I should take her and claim her before anyone else does. "Joshua Tanner at your service."

"Hi..." she answers, holding my gaze.

I already know I'm holding her hand for far too long, so I'm not surprised when Dad clears his throat and cuts me a crude stare to reiterate the warning he issued me. I release her hand and straighten up.

Although I've assumed professional mode, my mind is working overtime, conjuring up all the other ways I want her body.

Bent over the desk, on the desk, pressed up against the glass, and yes... she's wearing heels.

"Joshua, Giselle is one of the brightest attorneys we've ever hired. I think you'll enjoy working with her. I'm sorry I can't do it myself, but duty calls." Dad eyes me with seriousness, but his face softens when he looks at her. "Giselle, my son is the next best thing to me. He'll show you the ropes, and you'll be in good hands. I'll leave you two to get to know each other and discuss your plans. Let me know if either of you need anything."

"Of course," I say, and he gives me that look of caution again.

I may act like I can deal with him and the way he's arranged everything, but I know not to fuck with him. He's serious. He'll give Riley the opportunity to head the firm, and I'll just be here doing what I always do.

I love my job. That's the reason I'm so good at it. But I want more.

Doesn't mean I have to be a complete saint, though, in the process. How the fuck am I supposed to be the saint Dad wants me to be when I've already broken rule number one?

When Dad walks through the door, I return my attention to my little associate.

I didn't just have sex with her one time. It was six, and the seventh time would have been on the way if sleep hadn't taken me.

The fact that I woke up with my cock hard as fuck, wanting more, showed just how much she interested me.

And she still does.

"I... didn't know... who you were," she stutters.

My gaze drops to the gentle rise and fall of her chest, and I can't hide the hint of a smile that forces its way through when I recall how much fun I had playing with her tits.

My gaze climbs back up to her face, and I relish in the soft rose color that's tickling her cheeks.

"That's probably a good thing. Might not have had the adventurous night we had if you did." I grin.

We wouldn't have... or rather, she wouldn't. I still would. Had I known who she was last night, there's no fucking way I would have spent my night any other way after seeing her.

The first thing to intrigue me would have been that my little junior associate who's supposed to be Miss Goodie-Two-shoes from Stanford has the same taboo-as-fuck tastes as me. Even if it was her first time at The Dark Odyssey, she still went.

"Um... maybe," she breathes, still looking me over. It's shock that's taken her. I can see it in her eyes. While she's looking at me like she can't believe it's me, I'm looking at her and love that I got to see her in the sunlight.

The sunlight spilling through the floor-to-ceiling window picks out the different brown tones in her hair. Vibrant and soft around her angelic face.

This is a woman who's angelic, not Jennifer. Being the devil I am, I know, and I'm going to use it to my advantage.

"Maybe? So, you're not sure if you would have still slept with me as many times as you did if you knew I was your boss?"

She stares at me with those pretty brown eyes, and then she actually looks like she's going to faint.

"Oh my God... um, I'm sorry. I really didn't know, and the way I behaved last night was not a representation of me. I really want this job. I swear I'm good at what I do." Her eyes widen even more than they are as she continues to freak out.

I'm sure she means she's a good attorney, but I think she's also good with other things. Like using that mouth of hers. It fit perfectly around my cock, and I can't wait to be inside her again.

"Let me be the judge of that." I flick the coin over and hold it up in front of her. The color drains from her face as she looks from it to me. "I think things have taken a very interesting turn, don't you?"

I'm so bad. The sex club and the whole encounter from last

night isn't her. I watch and observe people very well. That's what makes me so good at what I do. My expertise at the firm here involves intellectual property, criminal law, and mergers. I prefer the first two because they always, always involve some piece of shit who decides he wants to screw people over. Just with one look I can usually tell someone's as guilty as fuck.

My analysis of Miss Giselle St. John is that she's the good girl with a wild side, and I want it.

She takes a step back, and her pretty mouth parts, worrying itself as she tries to think up some answer to give me.

"I don't know."

"You say that a lot. The thing is, I think you *do* know," I counter. "I think you know exactly what you want. What I don't know is why you don't just tell me. Like I think you know you didn't have to leave my bed this morning."

"I thought I was supposed to... Look, Josh. Last night was great, and I enjoyed myself. But I don't want to ruin things for us professionally."

I expected her to say that. I definitely did. It's a continuation of her mantra from earlier.

"*Professional...* interesting word. Very interesting word. For us though... not so much."

She just looks at me and blinks. "What do you mean?"

It's time to show her.

I love watching and showing all the fruits of my labor as a result of how observant I've been.

I have her coin. There's no rule that says when we should end, and the look in her eyes tells me I have permission. She still looks at me the same way she did last night. There hasn't been a single moment since she laid eyes on me this morning that she hasn't looked at me like she wants me.

Good for me. Good for her.

I step away from her, and she watches me as I walk up to the door and lock it so no one can come in and interrupt us.

I have five minutes, then I have a meeting.

Turning to face her confirms that permission. Desire glitters her eyes, along with lust. Both are accompanied by my personal favorite—*need*.

The need I see in those bright brown eyes of hers reflects exactly what I feel roiling inside me.

It's such a good thing that one of us isn't shy about what they want. It's probably a better idea too that it's me.

"Josh…" She says my name on the edge of a hushed whisper that sends the same thrill racing through me that I felt all of last night.

I make my way back to her, stepping purposefully into her personal space. Just like I thought she would, she steps back, still fighting temptation.

That's fine. The devil always recognizes weaknesses.

She just needs encouragement. That's what she needs.

"Giselle, I think it's safe to say that you got the induction into what it will be like to work with me last night. The good news is, we can use that for extra credits. But I think, just so there's no misunderstanding, I'll illustrate the fine print for you in greater details and show you exactly what I mean when I say *professional* won't work with us."

She takes an instinctive step back and hits the wall, exactly where I want her.

The contact startles her, and she looks me over with anticipation when I place my hands on the wall on either side of her.

I'm noticing very well how she's not fighting this, or disputing. I'm not hearing anything in the way of her protesting my forwardness. What I see is that curiosity from last night.

So… the first thing I do is push away from the wall, reach for the band holding her hair together in that ponytail, and allow her dark locks to tumble down her shoulders.

Against the wall, she looks as enticing as she did in the radiant light emanating from the wall at the club. It lit her up in blue, and the water flowing around her gave her a fairytale appearance. That was the first time that spark of pure need hit me in my gut.

"I mean this… I want your hair down because it's sexy as

fuck. You will wear it just like this every day." It's time to show her my true colors.

"What?"

"You heard me." I lean closer, take a lock of her silky hair in my hand, and allow the ends to curl around my thumb. "I want your hair like this. I like this too." I press my finger to her glossy pink lips, allowing her lipstick to smear my finger.

I hold up that finger, showing her the gloss, and she watches as I lick it off.

"My lipstick?"

"Any color will suit, but I like this one. And this..." It's the smell of her. Honey and flowers. I don't know which flower it is. It seems to be her natural scent. I lean further in and press my lips to her neck.

I won't kiss her lips because there's something about kissing her that steals my thoughts, and I need to have a clear mind about my meeting. It's the type where the room will be full of assholes. It's with one of Dad's clients who always tries to undermine me, so I always have to be ready.

The minute my lips brush her neck, I realize I was wrong. Kissing her here has the same damn effect as kissing her lips. It's her skin. No matter where I kiss on her body, it will have the same effect.

I have to fight the urge to devour her and pull myself away. I brush over her ear, and her breathing speeds up.

"I can't get the smell of you out of my head," I tell her, and she turns to look at me.

That heavy breathing turns me right back to those tits, and fucking hell, they look bigger than last night. I run my finger over her right breast, and she presses back into the wall, closing her eyes like she was dying for me to touch her tits.

"And these, Giselle..." I say, feeling my dick harden in my pants. Fuck, I wish I could be late. I'm dying to be inside her again, and I know she wants that too. I squeeze her breast and undo the little top button holding her breasts together so I can move away the cup of her bra, freeing the ample flesh from the tight restraint.

Her nipple is so tight the light pink rose tips have darkened. It pebbles beneath my touch when I take it between my thumb and forefinger.

Her eyes open, and she gazes at me. I can't resist the urge to play with her emotionally and physically.

I roll the pleading nipple between my fingers and smile down at her half-pleasure, half-pain expression.

It's sexy as fuck, and still I want more.

She moans, and my little associate does the sexiest thing by reaching for her other breast and massaging it. I just watch her and widen my grin. Looks like we're on the same page now.

Good.

"Giselle... do you want me to suck your tits?" I ask, raw and crass.

"Yes," she says, and I bend my head low to take her breast into my mouth.

I suck the one I'm holding and take over the job of massaging the other. There's no way I'm going to allow her to touch herself when I could do it.

I give her pleasure, and I'm grateful for where my office is situated.

It's the last on this floor and at the corner. Next to me is my own stationary closet that I alone have the keys for, and there's nothing but nature on the other side. The great view of the Chicago skyline and the river.

No one can see in, and no one can hear her as those moans fall from her lips.

Someone would have to be at my door to hear them, and the only man who'll be here today who could take that as a sign I'm up to no good is my father. I won't be seeing him again for the rest of the day.

I almost can't believe I get to indulge in this beauty again, and I'm pissed as fuck that I won't get to do all I want for the sake of time.

I suck on her, working the tips to life, and take out her other breast to get to work on that one too.

The sounds that come from her are unreal. I don't know how the hell I'm supposed to control myself. I want to continue my wild suckle to give her more pleasure. There's one more thing I want, however, and I will be selfish about it.

It will do for now since I can't take her right here up against this wall.

I move away from her breasts and leave her gasping for air, so I slide her skirt up her thighs, making it ride all the way up to her hips so I can get access to her panties.

She's wearing black lace today. *Perfect*. Against her creamy skin it screams sex and temptation.

I can't believe the scenario this could have been. Me meeting her and handing her the induction pack I prepped yesterday. I thought if I got past the Stanford attitude most people I'd met from there sported, I may take her for coffee.

This is so much better.

I get to my knees because I want to savor everything about what I plan to do to her next. It's the unadulterated version of the first time I did this to her. Seeing as this is all I will get right now, I won't be holding back.

I shove her panties to the side, lift her leg over my shoulder, relishing the feel of her heels grazing into my back. I then bury my face right into her pretty pussy. Her pretty pink lips are already wet and juicy, ready to be sucked and fucked.

I lick over her swollen clit and groan as the taste of her hits my tongue. It's that sweet floral taste to match her smell. I wish I could bottle it. *Fuck*, I have an idea that will shock her more than I already have.

I lick and suck, and her fingers smooth into my hair, urging me to continue giving her what she needs.

I'm very, very happy to oblige and offer my managerial support in whatever way she requires.

When I suck hard on her clit, eating her out like I'm actually feasting, she writhes against my face. Bucking and thrashing between me and the wall.

"Josh... I'm coming," she cries, and it's the most glorious sound I've ever heard.

I can never tire of hearing my name on her sexy mouth.

It sounds good there.

I suck harder and get lost in the taste of her as I stroke her skin, squeeze her ass, and suck her pussy like I want to take everything from her.

When she pushes against me and shudders, I know I have her where I want. Orgasm takes her, and her sweet nectar gushes into my mouth. I still my suckle to drink it up, and I don't move until it's all gone.

It's only then that I look up at her. Her hair is wild and luscious. Her cheeks flushed against glowing skin. She's panting, and the sight of her like this, with her tits hanging out of her shirt and her pussy right in my face, is enough for me to formulate the plan I want for us for the next three months.

Last night was something else.

But... just now...

Having her like this outside the club, with the taste of her in my mouth, is a whole other story.

I've just decided I want her.

I want her to be mine.

CHAPTER SIX

GISELLE

Holy shit...

I actually can't move.

I can barely breathe. He's looking at me, and I can't tell what he's thinking.

Fuck.... I can't even tell what *I'm* thinking.

My whole body heats again when he takes my leg from his shoulder and slides my panties down my legs.

It's like I've become a puppet. His puppet, and I know that I should do or say something, but want and need and desire have me under some spell.

At least my brain works enough to be shocked when he lifts my panties up to his nose and inhales them, then he pushes them into his pants pockets and stands up.

My mouth drops open at the sight, and I try to catch my breath.

"Spend the day getting to know your surroundings. You will work in here with me. I think that's best."

"What? I was given an office."

"Great... you'll be working in here with me," he repeats. "I'll see you at the club tonight at eight to discuss further working arrangements." He smiles, revealing that dimple again.

"The club? The Dark Odyssey?" I have to ask because this is all so unreal.

"Yes, ask for me at the door, and they'll take you up to my lounge."

He backs away, and I'm left looking on. He has a massive bulge straining his pants, but he grabs his jacket from the coat stand and hides it. He doesn't even look at me as he leaves.

The door clicks shut, and I'm alone in his office, wondering when it was I either went crazy or stepped into the Twilight Zone.

I look down and shriek when I see the state of me.

Quickly, I push my breasts back inside my bra, fix my shirt, and sit down on the sofa by the window to recover.

What the hell just happened?

Josh is my boss.

Josh, the man I met last night at The Dark Odyssey, the sex club, is my boss.

Josh is Joshua Tanner, Conrad Tanner's son.

Fuck.

How did this happen?

Now I'm here sitting in Josh's office wearing no panties.

No damn panties, and I'm thinking about later.

I bring my hand to my chest as my heart speeds up.

I need...

Rachel.

The thought of my best friend has me standing.

I stand and find the strength to move.

A very shocked Rachel stares back at me from the other side of the table.

We're at the coffeehouse near Tanners.

I made it to the little boutique nearby first before coming here so I could buy some panties.

I then made my way here to meet her, and I told her what happened. Everything.

This morning, I saw a text on my phone from her saying she hoped I had safe sex.

With everything that's happened, the fact that I didn't have anything near safe sex is the least of my worries.

Now I can't quite read her expression. I'm glad she stepped away from work to see me on such short notice, and I'm glad she didn't bring Jia. The two work together at Rachel's father's marketing and advertising firm.

This piece of news isn't for Jia's ears yet.

"Rachel, please say something, *anything*... I fucked up, and I think I may have to work somewhere else." That is something I'm not sure is even up for discussion.

Jesus Christ, I went through hell to get the job at Tanners. All the stuff with Dad drained me, and I know he'd be so ashamed if he knew I slept with a complete stranger. *And* I was ready to continue my activities with said stranger without another thought. Shit.

Rachel holds out her palms and releases a breath.

"Okay... Giselle, please don't hate me, but I think you called me so I can give you my advice. That is correct, right?" she asks carefully.

"Yes. I did. Rachel... I'm a mess. Maybe the shit with Kirk got to me more than I quite realized and screwed with me big time. Then Dad's death just left me feeling like... like I'm lost in the world. Maybe it gets to me more that he didn't get to see me make it. You know?"

Her shoulders slump, and she looks me over with sympathy.

Dad had stage four pancreatic cancer. He saw me graduate; he saw me pass the bar exams and all my academic achievements. He saw that at least, but he never saw me make it this far. He got sick after I passed the bar, and I took some time off to take care of him. I wanted him to see me make it as a lawyer, working in an actual law firm, but he died before he got the chance.

That was close to a year ago. I foolishly thought he was getting better, but from what the doctors said, it was clear he'd held back on telling me that there was no hope.

I wipe away a tear, and she pulls her chair closer so she can reach across the table and take my hand.

"Giselle, I'm sorry. Hearing about your father will always get to me. It makes me value mine, although ninety-five percent of the time he works my last nerve." When she pulls in a labored breath, I know something must have happened prior to her coming here. She frequently has run-ins with her father. It's because they're both as good as each other, and I think he secretly wishes her brothers could be as good as her. "You are not alone, and you are not lost. Like I said, I'm here for advice, and I think I know you well enough to know that you wouldn't do anything you didn't want to do."

My breath stills. "So, you're saying I want to screw my boss."

She laughs. "I'm just going to be blunt... *Don't you want to screw him?* Or rather, didn't you? I saw him, and he was hawt, Giselle. I can't imagine what the man must have looked like without the mask. My point is, this is weird, but it's wild. It's the wild you wanted."

"God, I didn't think it would be this wild. Rachel, this is crazy. Last night was last night, but this is work. I can't be some... mindless slave to sex at work. And it's like... well... I've never met anybody like him before. He just told me what to do. He didn't even ask me anything. He demanded and has this air of control that just makes me..."

"Want to submit?" She gives me a salacious smile, and embarrassment floods me when I nod.

This is how I've always been with her. Jia is close to me too, but she's a little too much for me. We all became close in high school, but I've known Rachel the longest.

"Well... men like that are a little different. This is definitely not going to be like Kirk."

No, I already knew that. Kirk spent his every waking hour trying to master the art of football. Josh seems to have spent his every waking hour mastering the art of how to provide maximum pleasure.

Just from the look of him you can tell he knows his way around the female body. He did things to me last night and made me feel things I didn't even know could be felt.

"What should I do, Rachel?" That's the question of the moment.

She smiles but gives my hand a gentle squeeze. "I think he likes you, and you should explore this. It's a nice surprise and one hell of a coincidence. I think you like him too, and you should definitely keep an open mind. Sometimes we can just have fun. Meet people for fun."

"What about work?"

She laughs again. "For you, Missy, I think work and play will be the same things for the next three months. Enjoy it, but... if you're that worried, why don't you just talk to him about it? Make a few demands of your own. That's what I would do if it were me. There would be no way on earth that I'd allow a man like that to slip away from me. It's so much the better that he wants to play at work. Come on, Giselle, a little fun with a gorgeous man will not harm you. Will it?"

I try to bite back a smile, but it comes out anyway. "Maybe not... but it's just weird. It's different."

"It's sexy and confident. *Daring.*" She nods. "See where it goes, but... only if you want to."

I'm noticing how she's not saying anything about my discomfort. Again, that's because she knows me. On this occasion, she seems to know me a little better than I do myself.

She seems to have already factored in that I won't allow my discomfort to take precedent over my curiosity.

That's what takes me right back to the club for the second night in a row.

Curiosity.

I admit, though, that there's a little something else that I don't want to acknowledge, because when I do, I'm a goner.

It's desire.

I've never felt it like this before, and in such a way that it makes me forget reason and logic.

Then again, maybe I just think I'm forgetting *reason and logic*. Where does it say that the wild, reckless way I've been with Josh isn't within reason or logic? It's me. It's that part of me I was trying to push aside to bring the sexy out, and the confidence.

I'm great at work, but socially? No.

Tonight, though, I may just shock myself for night number two.

I'm wearing black this time. A black slip with lace at the edge over the top to accentuate my cleavage. Because I'm supposed to be going to see Josh, I've opted not to wear a mask.

It's a different receptionist this time, and when I give his name, curiosity enters her eyes. I know the Tanners are rich, but I didn't get the impression that Conrad Tanner was into anything this... *wild*.

His only son, on the other hand, yes.

Today, I did the research I should have done weeks ago when I first got my offer letter to work for Tanners. I googled Josh, and Jesus Christ, he made the devil look like a patron saint.

The Internet had enough gossip and stories to keep the tabloids running on steam with just him and his extracurricular activities. All the articles involved him on some sexual conquest with models, actresses, socialites, and other women like that.

The more I read, the more I realized why I knew nothing. It's because over the last two years—I'd put it down to two years—my life has been very different.

I've barely read a magazine.

My father died, and my boyfriend, who I thought I'd be with forever, broke up with me. I think I could be forgiven for not keeping up with the latest playboy billionaire who happens to be my boss.

Like last night, I hand over my coat and keep the little mini purse wrapped around my wrist. It still has his coin inside.

I didn't get another.

I'm led by the guard up to the second floor, where we pass one of the cubicles holding a man and two women—twins—having a threesome.

Again, I find myself looking. It's shock that makes me look, and I wonder how I'd feel if that were me. And with family? I don't think I would like to be shared or have to share.

We continue to a private bar area that's on a raised platform. Across from the bar is an elegant sofa that looks as classy as the rest of the club.

"He'll meet you here," the man says.

"Thank you," I answer, and he leaves me.

I move over to the balcony and watch the scenery below of the people dancing, having fun, and having sex. I can't believe I'm here again tonight. It was so packed last night, and it's probably even more crowded tonight.

I get the feeling that a place like this is always packed, even with the hefty price tag. Our ticket last night was a hundred dollars. I got a text earlier in the day from Josh—who now has my number—letting me know that everything had been paid for. I was just to get here and meet him.

I set my purse down on the little table and continue to watch the party people. The music's just changed to a live mix I don't recognize but sounds good. It's fast but sensual and sexy.

Warm hands slide around my waist at that moment.

I look around and see him. Face bent low to my ear, his warm breath tickles my skin like a whisper of desire.

"We haven't danced yet," he says, and I turn to face him.

"No... we haven't," I reply, and we start moving together.

Almost immediately, that need to lose control sweeps through me, just from his touch and his closeness.

He towers over me, dominant and breathtaking in his white

button-down shirt and black pants, his eyes on me. He isn't wearing a mask either, and up here, the light is brighter, so I can see that predatory look in his eyes quite clearly.

I haven't recovered yet from last night, let alone this morning, and I'm not sure what to expect from tonight.

Rachel was right, though, about a few things.

I never do anything I don't want to, and I like him.

I think he knows that last part.

CHAPTER SEVEN

GISELLE

"You came," he states as I step forward.

"Did I have a choice?" I answer, and he moves closer.

He leans forward, like he's going to kiss me, but stops a breath away, just hovering by my lips. Instinct tells me he wants me to kiss him and only met me halfway.

The quirk of his brow lures me forward, so I move. I close the space between us and press my lips to his.

We kiss, and our tongues tangle and chase. It's him who pulls back first and gives me that wicked smile.

"You always have a choice, Giselle St. John. Like you proved just now." He smiles with triumph. "Don't resist."

"I'm not," I lie, and I'm sure he can see straight through me.

"Good, because I plan to have a lot more fun with you tonight." He smirks, studying me.

"I thought we were working." Of course, I knew we wouldn't be. I just want to see his reaction, which is exactly as I expected.

He smiles and pulls me closer, pressing me up against him so I can feel the bulge of his cock against my stomach.

"*Really?*" he asks, catching my face again.

He holds my face up as we sway to the music, and then he releases me and walks around me slowly. He stops behind me, and I glance over my shoulder to find him checking out my ass again.

His gaze runs up my thighs, and he surprises me by moving the hem of my slip up my legs and up my hips, exposing my panties.

"I'm wearing panties," I tell him, putting forth my voice before he does anything more to steal it away.

He chuckles and allows the slinky material to float from his fingers. "It's wishful thinking. Can't blame a guy for that with a sexy-as-fuck woman like you." That's the second time he's said something like that to me.

"You think I'm sexy as fuck?"

He chuckles and straightens up. "Yes, don't you?"

"I try." Best to say that because there's no way I've ever thought of myself in that way.

"You don't have to try, trust me." He presses his hand to the edge of my hip and pulls on my panties through the slip. "I'll be having that pair tonight too. You smell different."

My God... I raise my brows. I don't know how to be with him.

"How do I smell?" *Why did I ask that?*

That question gave him the invite to sniff my neck. Oh, but he doesn't just stop there; he licks over the skin and inhales, like he's smelling something to savor.

"It's citrus. Something with a hint of orange. Like Sanguinello oranges, freshly picked."

I'm impressed. That's actually the name of my new shower gel. "It's stuff I bathe with."

"Wonderful, so your pussy will smell the same." The rawness of his words makes my pussy clench with need. It's clear what he plans to do with me tonight. It's clear he wants a repeat of last night, and damn me... I want it too.

I've known this man for a little over twenty-four hours, and all I can think of when he looks at me the way he is and the way he touches me is that I can't wait for him to be inside me.

He takes hold of me again, and we sway to the sexy music that moves us. He stays behind me, and we move like our bodies were made to dance together. Each move is electric and scandalous. He makes sure that as I wiggle my hips, he's grinding against me, moving with me too.

I forget where we are.

I forget that people are watching us. There are people down below on the dance floor who can see us, and the bartender behind the private bar is just there across from us.

These types of movements are best reserved for the bedroom and definitely not done with your boss.

I forget everything and remember that the club is like one big bedroom, just with more people. It's not the creepy, seedy type of vision you'd get when you think of a sex club.

It's fantasy.

Everything about it has that dreamlike feel, except it's real.

It's not long before Josh's hands travel up my waist to cup my breasts, and as he does, I lean back into him and turn my head up so we can kiss.

While our tongues work each other, he gives my breasts a good feel, and I do my best to move over his cock with my ass so I can pleasure him too. I'm different from last night. So very different. More confident and sure about what I want.

It's like I've become that woman I wanted to be when I first stepped through the doors.

Confident, sexy, daring.

I'm here now. I'm here now with him. I must be because I'm not resisting or doing anything of the sort when he guides me over to the sofa and takes off my slip.

The slip has a built-in bra, so all I'm left in is my panties and heels. The way he wants me.

A wicked smile spreads across his face. My mouth waters when he pulls off his shirt, revealing that fantasy body which fits in perfect with the dreamlike feel of the place. In one quick second, he sheds the rest of his clothes, and my eyes land on his perfectly erect cock.

I'm that woman again, because I reach down and take it like I'm supposed to and love the groan that leaves his lips as I run my hands over his smooth length.

I start pumping, and his cock strains upward, growing in my hands. He clamps a firm hand on my wrist, stopping me from going further.

"You get to play with that later. I need to be inside you now," he says.

I giggle when he grabs my waist and pulls me down into his lap as he sits on the sofa. I straddle him, and he fills his palms with the cheeks of my ass, squeezing, then moving my panties aside so he can push his cock into me.

It's only when he enters my pussy and I arch my back that I see a couple below watching us, and my awareness returns to me again.

All that time I touched him, I got lost in the fantasy. Now, reality has creeped back in. I'm having sex in public, and people are watching, but… it doesn't stop me.

Josh smooths his hand up my back as he moves faster into me, fucking me. His hand glides up to the back of my neck, and I focus on him.

"Look at me, baby, focus on us and the movement. You'll enjoy it more if you do that," Josh says.

"Okay…" I stutter and press into him as he squeezes my hips and starts fucking me hard.

His cock pulses in my pussy, and my walls tighten. I'm already on the verge of coming, and I know I won't last.

"You're even more beautiful when you get lost in pleasure," he says, pulling my head right up to his. "Give yourself to me, Giselle, stop resisting."

I didn't realize I was, but I know what he means. It was the hesitation of everything. Being here and being seen.

I smooth my hands up his jaw, running my fingers over the scruff, and I kiss him.

I kiss him hard, showing him how much I want him, and I

get sucked into the fantasy again. I allow him to take me. I give myself to him and hand over that logic I so often rely on.

When his cock pulses inside me, that tension that was coiling deep within my groin pushes up, rising higher and higher like a pressure cooker, and when it reaches the top, it explodes, and I throw my head back, crying out into the release that takes me. It's scandalous and raw, like us.

He pounds harder and faster, rutting into me until he blows hot cum up into my passage. I feel it, and it feels good.

He then reclaims my lips, and I know then that tonight isn't going to be like last night at all. It's going to be more. So much more. More of this insane frenzy that's come over me to be with this man.

It's the sun that wakes me again.

Just like yesterday.

Yesterday, I freaked because I didn't want to be late for my first day of work, and today I'm...

Well, I'm not sure yet. I open my eyes, forcing them to stay open against the bright sunlight.

I'm in bed, that same bed from yesterday, but Josh isn't asleep next to me.

He's sitting across the room by the window.

The window is open, and he's in a chair wearing just his boxers, smoking a cigar while he flicks through some files.

He is the one who looks sexy as fuck, and oh my God, last night was even wilder than the night before.

We went to one of the themed rooms. It was one that was futuristic with those fluorescent lights. It was supposed to be something sci-fi related, but we didn't get to the part of any kind of role play. He just liked the way I looked in the lights.

Then we came here, and it turns out there's a hot tub outside the room on the terrace. That was where we had the most fun. I didn't know sex in water could be so much fun.

I didn't know *I* could be so much fun, or have it.

Now it's daylight, and we're here. I'm here, and I'm supposed to be at work soon. Except he's here too.

He looks across at me, and I sit up, pulling the covers up to my breasts and allowing my hair to drift over my shoulders.

"Morning," I say, trying to sound cool and casual.

"Wow..." he replies as he continues to study me.

I find myself laughing. "Are you kidding? I probably look like a cave woman. It's you who looks *wow*." He does.

I don't know anyone who can pull off the just-got-out-of-bed hair look with such suave and sexiness.

"Thank you, but I'm not joking. Or being nice. I don't think lies help anybody, so you can trust that I'll never lie to you."

That gets me. I shouldn't be thinking about us as anything other than whatever we are, but it means a lot to hear him say that.

Kirk lied all the time. He lied to me all the time, and getting that sensation that he was cheating on me was awful. I remember when I flat out asked him, and he told me he wasn't. I knew it was a lie.

Josh straightens up, pulling my attention back to him. He sets the file down on the window bay and takes a draw on the cigar.

"What is that?" I ask, referring to the file.

"Work. I was supposed to bring myself up to speed on my new associate a few days ago, but I didn't."

"Why not?"

"I heard that she went to Stanford, and I decided I didn't like her." He allows the cigar to dangle between his thumb and forefinger.

"What's wrong with Stanford?"

He chuckles. "What's right with it, baby? I've never met anyone who went there who didn't make anybody else who studied law feel inferior. And fuck, they aren't nearly as good as most from Harvard."

This is clearly a Joshua Tanner observation, because I've never heard anyone say that.

"Did you go to Harvard?"

"I didn't. I went to Georgetown, like my father and all the men in my family who are lawyers. But I would have chosen Harvard as my second choice. I doubt, though, that their strict ways would have been suitable for someone like me." He puts the cigar out on the ashtray in front of him, and a look of seriousness washes over his face. "Come here."

I start to get up and take the sheet to cover me, but he holds up his hand, stopping me.

"Leave the sheet and walk over to me naked," he commands, and I obey.

I allow the sheet to fall from me, and I slide off the bed.

My nipples harden from the way he looks at me from head to toe.

When I get to him, he pulls me into his lap, and I glance out the window just to make sure no one can see us. See me. Inside the club is one thing, but being seen naked by people on the street is another.

I'm grateful when I see that we're so high up in the penthouse suite that no one can see in. The height of the window and angle that we're sitting in hides us well too.

His eyes drop to my pussy, and he rubs his finger over my already swollen clit.

"So... I'm wondering this..." he says, smoothing his hands up my waist. "I'm already suspicious of anyone from Stanford, and usually, I'd have a person checked out so thoroughly I'd know what they had for dinner over the course of a week. Yet... except for this file, I'm more intrigued to hear more about you from you."

I tuck my hair behind my ear and hold his gaze. What can I tell him that won't sound boring?

I bite the inside of my lip. "I'm afraid I just work really hard. There's not much you'd find outside those files, and over the course of a week, I tend to eat Mexican food. I like it. And it helps that it's easy to prep."

I barely had a week before I had to start work at Tanners. Prior to starting, I was at a medium-sized firm called Barkers. I wanted to have a week to myself to plan properly and get some rest, but since I needed the money, I carried on working.

"They worked you hard at Barkers?" he asks.

"Yeah, it was busy, and I just had no time. So, Mexican it was in the , with a film."

God, I sound boring. I should stop talking.

"What film, baby..."

"You want to know what film?"

"Yeah, tell me."

"I ...love old films. Classics like *Casablanca* or *Some Like It Hot*. Anything like that." I press my lips together and feel a blush creep into my cheeks. "My dad used to love them, and he got me hooked when I was a kid. It was our thing. We'd just watch TV when he came back from work. He worked a lot."

"What did he do?"

"He was a teacher. He taught math. Sorry... this is so boring."

"No... it's definitely not boring. I need the picture of what your life's like."

"Why? You seem to hate anyone from Stanford," I ask playfully.

"You changed my mind, and in case you didn't notice, I'm a little obsessed with you."

"Obsessed?" I have to ask because of the fascination that takes me. I'm intrigued that someone like him can be obsessed with me.

"Yes... so, I've finally come up with an offer for you."

"An offer?" I ask.

"Yes. I like the fun we're having far too much. How about we continue this for the next three months? We start the day in the office, and we'll see where we end up."

"And, um... will there be actual work involved?" I ask tentatively.

He smiles. "Yes. I'll teach you everything I know. In three months, you'll be signed off as an attorney, and you'll be able to work anywhere in Tanners, which means anywhere, really, with the prestige our name carries. And for fun...." He lingers on that last word.

"What?"

"I want you. Three months... for that time, I want you completely. You give yourself to me the way you did last night, and more. I want you for three months. Your body to do whatever I want, anytime I want, and in whatever way I want."

My breath stills.

I want to ask if this is the kind of thing where if I say no, I won't get what I want... but I don't.

I can tell from the look in his eyes that he's set out his offer the way he has on purpose because he can see I want him too.

Darkness lurks in the depths of his eyes that's as sexy as it is dangerous. Darkness, mingling with greed, need, and hunger. It robs any form of protest from my mind.

"What say ye, Giselle St. John? Remember... you have a choice." The smile that dances on his lips pulls at my insides.

"Do I get you too?" I hear myself ask.

He chuckles. "You want me? A nice girl like you wants me? Sweetheart, don't you see I'm the devil?"

I run my fingers over the tattoo he has inked over his heart. It's the Japanese character for water.

"I want you too," I tell him.

"Then yes. Give me an answer, Giselle. I want to hear it."

"Yes."

CHAPTER EIGHT

JOSH

The good girl and the fucking devil...
    The thought makes my damn mouth water even though I'm drinking coffee.
    Matt and I are in the break room at the office. He presses the button on the coffee machine to make his usual cappuccino while he continues to regale me with his recount of the craziness he's been up to for the last few days.
    Officially, it was a business trip, but my best friend is just a little better than me when it comes to thinking up wild sexual adventure. He's been my partner in crime for as long as I can remember. So, I'm not surprised to hear how he turned that business trip to Phoenix into a sex marathon with the sassy, leggy dark-haired attorney at Porters he's always battling in court.
    Her name is Elena. With her Brazilian beauty, she has that Latina presence about her that has the man staring after her like a dog. It's his downfall every time, and the worst thing is, she knows it. I've been watching this back-and-forward shit play out between them for two years, and it's so obvious in the courtroom when they argue.

One judge even told them to get a room. I'm so glad they did.

"It was just fucking explosive, Josh, but now that we're back, I don't know what the hell to do." He sips on his drink and looks at me like he actually wants my advice.

I shake my head at him and laugh.

This is the first time I'm seeing him since he left last week. He's aware of my debacle with Dad and Riley, but I haven't informed him yet of the newest complication. We've spoken on the phone, but I always prefer to talk to him about anything like... well, what I'm up to in person. It's just the way I am.

"Christ... I think I should ask her out. I should, shouldn't I?" Matt says, prodding for an answer.

I glare at him because if he doesn't know that's obviously the next logical thing to do, he's more hopeless than I am of finding that special someone. "Matt, you've been drooling over the woman for years. Stop being a pansy-ass bitch and take her out."

"Okay... where though? Restaurants might not be her thing. She's an excellent cook."

I just stare at him. "Matt, since when does a woman who's an excellent cook say no to going to a restaurant?"

"Oh God, what the fuck's wrong with me?"

He is displaying what I imagine happens when a playboy meets his match. He doesn't know what to do with himself.

"Man... I have my own problems." I wince and think of my little associate who's had me staring after her like a dog for the last few days.

"Shit, I'm sorry. I've just been talking. How's it been going? You haven't said. How's the associate? I still can't believe your old man is making you train her."

"Yeah, about that..." The minute I say that, he stills mid-sip because he knows what I'm going to say.

"My God, Josh, you slept with her already?" he hisses and looks over his shoulder to check if we're still alone.

We are. So, I fill him in on the latest crazy to take me.

The look on his face is surprise mixed with some element of

expectation. I understand both. He's not surprised because I'm with Giselle the way I am, or that I met her at The Dark Odyssey. Matt and I are always there hanging out in the playboy lounge with our other friends. We all met in college.

We stuck together because we're the most similar, and we meet up with the other guys a couple of times a month at the club just to touch base and have fun. What he's surprised by is me doing this with her in these dangerous times when my fucking future is on the line.

I have to admit that it surprises me too.

"Well, hell, Josh." He sighs.

"I know. It's crazy, right? But like fuck am I going to allow my dad to treat me like a child."

Since Giselle and I made that deal, we've spent every night the same. It's been five days now. Today is Friday. We met Sunday night. I woke up with her in my arms this morning and didn't leave the suite before taking her again. In the bed and then the shower. I don't care what anyone says, I'm having my fun with her. As long as Dad doesn't find out, I'm good. My work is my work, and the merits of me getting that job should only be based on work and nothing else.

Matt gives me a narrowed look and looks me over. Then something enters his eyes, like curiosity mixed with interest.

"Josh," he states.

"What?"

"You're taken with her, aren't you?" he observes.

"What do you mean?"

"Josh... the guy I know would have done everything possible to focus on what he needs to for the job. But you seem more focused on her," Matt says, shaking his head.

As he says that, I recall myself telling Giselle I was obsessed with her.

"You know how I feel about this shit with Riley."

"And yet you've just commissioned your own fuck toy." He widens his eyes at me and gives me an incredulous glare. "Didn't your old man all but tell you to keep your dick in your pants with this one?" He nods his blond spikey head.

"My fucking dick had already been inside her several times before I realized she was the same woman I was supposed to keep away from."

He shakes his head at me.

"It's fun and games, man. All fun," I add.

Fun...As I look ahead through the glass wall, I see my little associate walking down the corridor that leads to her office.

All I have to do is look at her, and the ideas come.

Matt sees her too and witnesses the sexiest thing about her. She's completely oblivious to the effect she has.

She smiles at Sheila, the receptionist, and continues into her office. Not knowing that I'm looking at her like I want to devour her.

"I'm guessing that's her?" Matt says, and I look back to him.

"Yeah."

"Fun?" He quirks a brow.

"Lots of fun."

———

It's fun, but I'm going to be subtle with her today. She'll need me to go easy on her before later.

I have plans about what I want to do with that body of hers.

We just got a new case. It's an intellectual property dispute. I noticed that she got really excited about it.

We're supposed to be negotiating with our client, who wants his designs protected. The other company wants him to provide full disclosure for his work.

Giselle sits across from me, looking over the documents Sheila brought in with sheer fascination. I can't help but stare at her just for that. I've never known anybody to get so excited over paperwork.

"This is your thing," I note, and her gaze flicks up to meet mine. "You like the intellectual property cases?"

"Yeah... I really want to specialize in it. It's the area that made me want to become a lawyer."

Interesting. "Me too."

"Yeah?"

"My dad loves it. That's his thing, and when he'd talk about it, it really interested me. What was it for you?" I like hearing about her.

"My dad too, except it was a show we were watching. We liked *Perry Mason*," she laughs, and it's the best sound ever. "We watched a lot of TV."

"That's okay. Different things inspire us. Does your dad still teach?"

The smile recedes from her face, and she sighs. "No, he died last year. It's why I... took that break of sorts."

My hands stills, and I feel bad that I've known her for close to a week and didn't know that.

"I'm sorry," I say and shuffle to straighten up.

"That's okay. He had cancer, and I guess I should be glad I had him for as long as I did. My mom... wasn't around much," she explains.

Maybe I should have had her checked out. I feel off for not knowing this, but having her tell me feels better.

"Come here," I tell her, and she gets up. She makes her way over to me, and I pull her down on my lap.

"Josh, what if someone comes in and sees us?" She looks nervously at the door, which isn't locked.

"Do I look like I care?" I smirk. Truthfully, I do care because Dad could indeed come through that door, or Riley, but I want this with her. I slip my arm around her tiny waist and hold her to me. "I'm going to let you handle this case," I tell her, and her eyes go wide.

"Me?" She actually points at herself.

"Yeah, you," I say with a firm nod. "Think of it as a test. Your first assignment."

"But they're big clients."

She's right. Our client is Mark Frontableu, owner and CEO

of Spark Inc., a games development company, and the company who is merging with his is Logstrick, owners of a host of technological devices.

"What does that matter? Your knowledge and expertise are what is needed here. Mark needs us—you—to advise him on the best course of action here. Clearly, the crux of the matter is, he doesn't want to piss off Logstrick, who are offering him a very sweet deal considering he's going bust."

That was the problem, although no one has said it. I have a great PI who checks things out for me, and he knows when shit doesn't look right but the clients are holding off on being up front.

"You think he's going bust?" she asks.

"Yes," I answer and lean closer. "It's intuition. And the numbers don't look right to me. The man has his back against the wall, so he's the little guy in this scenario. He wants to save his ass so he can keep doing what he does, but he wants to save that thing that's most precious to him." I phrase it like that because I know exactly what I would do here, and I want to see where her head is at.

"His knowledge of what only he can do," she puts in and nods.

"See, you are different to most from Stanford."

She smirks. "Josh, there are some nice people who went to Stanford. It's really not as bad as you think. I loved it there."

I frown. "Woman... tread softly. First, you get me to like you, and now, you want me to like the whole pack of them."

She holds my gaze and runs her fingers over my chest. "You like me?"

The question throws me off guard, but then what did I expect from my comment?

"I like you enough to allow you to handle the case."

"Maybe you won't like me so much if I tell you that I think Mark should hold on to his rights."

I smile at her. That's the very thing I was going to suggest. "And why do you think he should do that?"

"They're merging with him as a company. Business is business for monetary sake. If he wants his ideas to be his only and not classed as part of the newly-formed company, then he's within his rights to. Sure, if he wants to share his trade secrets with them on new projects after the merger, that's probably more acceptable, but I don't think this is."

"*Wow...*" I state, and she looks nervous.

"Is that a good *wow* or... something else?"

"It's good. I agree with you. Besides, if they want him that badly, they'll agree to his terms. I don't think he has anything to worry about, so go over what you think is best to protect his rights, meet with him and discuss it. If he's happy with that, I'll set up a mediation meeting and sit in with you."

She smiles down at me. "Thank you so much. I really appreciate it."

"That's okay. Go... take a break, wrap up, and go home early. I have something interesting planned for later."

The spark that enters her eyes hardens my cock.

"What is it?"

"You'll see."

"Don't I get a clue?"

I lean into her lips and kiss her. "The clue is, I think you'll love it."

"That's not a clue."

"When you get to the club, you'll see what I mean," I answer and run my fingers over her breasts.

She shuffles over my cock, and I wish now that I'd closed the door.

Damn it though. I have another meeting in fifteen minutes, and it's in the other building. It's one I can't be late for.

I kiss her again, making that be enough to satisfy my need for her.

"Go... before I get myself in trouble."

She slips off my lap and straightens her clothes.

"I want you in red tonight. I'll send something to your house," I say.

"Is this what it will be like for the next three months? What if I wanted to wear yellow? Would you terminate me?"

I lean back, liking this challenging side of her.

"Do you want to wear yellow, Giselle?"

"I might have."

I stand and catch her face, but she seems used to me now and just melts into the hold.

"You will wear what I send over tonight and wear yellow tomorrow."

"Tomorrow is Saturday. The office is closed."

"Like fuck... the fucking office is closed, but the club is still open."

"So, you want to see me on Saturdays too? During my free time when we aren't working?" She gives me a tempting smile, and I find myself liking this far too much.

"Yes," I answer, and satisfaction twinkles in her eyes.

"Okay."

I release her, and she steps back.

"Eight at the club. Ask for me, and they'll take you to me."

"Aren't we going to the lounge?"

"No." She's perceptive. I get the feeling she knows I have a dominant personality, so she won't be too surprised when she sees what I have planned for later.

"I'll see you later, then."

As she saunters away, I watch her go, and Matt's words come to my mind.

The scent of her lingers as she leaves, and I find that all I can think of is her.

I'm taken and obsessed.

I can't wait to get my hands on her tonight, and tomorrow when we wake, we don't have to leave to go anywhere.

I plan to have her all to myself, starting tonight.

CHAPTER NINE

GISELLE

"Holy shit." Rachel gasps, holding up the red baby doll negligee Josh has sent over for me to wear later.

That's exactly what I said when I opened up the package. It came from Victoria's Secret, and it was hand delivered by a personal shopper from the store.

Rachel came over for an early dinner I decided to make so I could catch up with her. She didn't sound too good on the phone yesterday, and since she's the kind of friend to try to weather her personal problems by herself, I thought this little session would help in some way.

I never meant to make it about me.

Rachel looks from me to the negligee, lips parted the same blood-red color as the piece of garment Josh wants me to wear later.

I say *piece of garment* because the whole thing is just lace. Lace, and it's crotchless.

See-through lace gathers the top and then flows down the bodice. The only thing that's not see-through is the ribbon trimming the edges, but really, does that even count?

I sigh and throw myself down on the sofa.

"Rachel, what the hell am I getting myself into?" I ask her because really, what am I doing? This is five days in, and look at me.

What sort of relationship is this where it's just so physical?

She smiles at me and joins me on the sofa.

"I know it's crazy, but I like it. I like this for you because it's so wild. You've never had this. *Fuck*, I've never had this, and I've done a lot. Trust me, just go with the flow." She nods with firm determination.

"Go with the flow, and what if it leads me somewhere I don't want to be? He's just so unpredictable, and I... like that."

"Why is that so bad?" She gives me a disbelieving glare.

"It's bad, Rachel, because we're two people meeting up for sex, and it feels like there's something more, but I know that realistically, there isn't. It's not real. It's physical and nice and adventurous, and I'm experiencing all the feels you get when you get into a relationship, but it just feels so out of control. What happens when it burns out? He's used to this, but I'm not."

She looks at me and studies my expression.

"You do like him..." she points out with a little smile.

"Yeah... I do. It's nice to be adored, and it's nice that he wants to know me." I like it when he starts asking me questions about myself.

"That's a good thing. It shows he's interested in more about you outside of the sex."

"It is just sex though, and I think the next three months are going to be very interesting."

"Sure, but those parts are the foundation for anybody, even if this is fun."

"You know... the little time I've spent with Josh is so much more effective than all the time I spent with Kirk. Kirk barely wanted to do what I wanted. I think he thought I was boring from the beginning."

He hated my classic films and anything to do with law. He

hated that I was so academic. I think what he liked was the look of me. That's it. He jumped ship the minute he could do better.

"What's important is this exploration, no matter who you're with."

I nod, agreeing. The exploration is something I'm liking. It was, however, hard talking about Dad today, like it always is, but it's worse talking about Mom.

I'm glad Dad thought I barely remembered her long before he died. The truth was, I remembered all there was to remember about her, and I still do, including the day she left us. I was nine, and I remember her getting in a car with some man who looked like the rough stuff, who threatened to kill Dad, and then they drove away. That was it. While Dad and I never spoke about it, I knew what happened. Mom was pregnant when she left. As I grew older, I did the math for myself and knew she cheated, got pregnant with that guy's baby, and left us. I never saw her again and never heard of her. I don't talk about her, so me just mentioning her today to Josh was unlike me.

I could see, though, that he would have asked about my mother if we were talking about my father.

"I'm crazy," I chuckle when I see her watching me. "You probably think I'm crazy. I've known this guy for less than a week, and here I am, doing the worrying thing, ready to shoot myself in the foot because this whole arrangement of ours is based on wild sexual fun we have while living out our fantasies at The Dark Odyssey."

She shakes her head. "No. I don't think it's crazy. You just see something you like and want it. There's no harm in that. Well, unless you're me and you're still just as crazy over your dad's best friend as you were when you were five."

My jaw drops. Right… so, that's what's up with her.

I would have guessed if I'd known Dante was back in town.

I know this story, and it's not a good one because I have no idea what to tell her when it comes to Dante Lombroso, Rachel's dad's best friend, who is twenty years older than her.

He's also about to get married.

"Rachel..." I begin, and my voice trails off when she looks at me with huge sad eyes.

First, I just thought it was a crush. Dante is absolutely gorgeous, and there's no woman alive who wouldn't think it. He has the kind of looks that only get better with age, and the last time I saw him was at her parents' anniversary, where he announced his engagement. That was nearly a year ago.

"I know... you don't have to say it. It's stupid. It's stupid because I can't be with him. I just need to get to the part where I kick that fantasy to the curb. Give it a good kick because the ship has sailed into the great beyond."

"What happened?" I ask. Something must have happened for her to bring him up. She's seemed fine outside of the times she's seen him. She dates and gets up to her wild adventures with her guys, and we only ever mention Dante in times like these when she starts sulking for one reason or another.

"He's coming back to Chicago with his fiancée. They're gonna settle down here, so that means he'll be working at the same place as me. I'll see him every day. Dad's planning to slow down so he can spend more time with Mom, and well... that means Dante may be in charge. It won't be me, and that's cool. I'm not cut up about that. I'm fine with what I'm doing. What I'm not that thrilled about is seeing him and knowing I can't be with him... *ever*."

I bite the inside of my lips.

"Rachel, I'm gonna try to be you and give the advice I think you'd give me. You'd say to move on, or..." I hold my breath because Rachel's advice is always something with a twist of some spark to get a person thinking. Just like how she told me to give this thing with Josh a chance. Another friend wouldn't do that. Jia would be in agreement, and has been, but she wasn't as gentle as Rachel in understanding things from my perspective.

"Or what?" She raises her shoulders. "There's an or?"

"Yes, remember, I'm pretending to be you. So, you'd say he's getting married, so respect it and move on, but... if he never knew how you felt and perhaps he felt the same way, how would he have known there was a chance?"

I would have completely erred on the side of caution and accept that that ship really had gone to the great beyond. But because she looks so sad, I thought I'd mention that. *And...* it seems to work.

"Thank you. That's good advice, Giselle. It's something to think about, although I think I may just have to see my dream guy get married to someone else. I may be ballsy, but I don't know if I can be that brave. How about we focus on you again? I'll try to get over my grief."

"Okay, let's eat some of that chocolate we got last time." I have a cupboard full of it. It was from my breakup with Kirk. Every time the girls came to the house, they brought chocolate.

"Okay, let's do that. I'll help you with your makeup," she declares, standing up.

I guess I'm probably going to have to leave in a while. It's six thirty. To get to the club for eight, I'll have to leave at seven fifteen.

"Thank you." I return the smile, still feeling crazy because I'm so excited to see Josh I can hardly contain myself.

I'm excited and nervous as hell.

What does he have planned for later?

I get the feeling it's something that will shock me.

I was right.

I knew it had to be something to shock me more than he already had, and more than I'd already shocked myself.

My mouth falls open when the guard ushering me to see Josh leads me into the sex dungeon. Josh is waiting for me inside. He's talking it up with another man dressed in period wear. Period wear as in Victorian gothic style. The man looks like a pirate too with the black eyeliner around his eyes.

They're sitting opposite each other. Seeing the man makes

me curious, but what turns my attention away from him is a woman curled up on the floor in between his legs with a collar around her neck.

The collar has a lead on it, and the man is holding the lead in one hand and stroking her head with his free one.

Instantly, I know what they are. She must be a sub, and he's her Dom.

My eyes went straight to them, and I was so absorbed in looking at them that I didn't fully look around the room.

It's the sounds of sexual pleasure that catch my attention and make me look in the direction it comes from. It's coming from a woman with her arms attached to chains on the wall ahead of us. She cries out in pleasure as a man fucks her into the wall. Both are naked.

The room is brighter than the rest of the club and more like a gathering setting.

I scan various equipment people into BDSM use and a host of kinky people having sex before I notice that Josh has stood up and is making his way over to us.

The guard leaves me when Josh reaches us and takes my hand.

His smile is what I focus on, although I know my whole face is possibly as red as what I'm wearing. I'm wearing the negligee he got me under a silky black robe. I'd thought to take off the robe before, believing we'd be going somewhere private-ish like his lounge, but now I'm glad I didn't.

He smiles when he sees my face.

"Don't worry. We won't be doing anything too wild," he states, giving me a little kiss.

"What will we be doing?" I ask. My voice quivers, and he slips his arms around me.

"Nothing you don't want to do. Come, let me show you." He leads me past the people, but I can't stop looking. There's a woman bent over a man's lap being spanked hard, and the look on her face is complete pleasure. There's another woman on her knees with one guy pounding into her from behind while she sucks the cock of the guy in front of her.

I notice her ass is red, and she too is wearing a leather collar around her neck.

This is all about pain and pleasure. Everyone looks so engrossed in what they're doing, and the ones who notice me looking can tell straight away that I'm not used to it.

Something about all of it though... from the people having sex on the main parts of the club to these people inside, has that element of freedom. It calls to me.

Josh leads me through a large oak door, and we enter a corridor where it's just us. My heels click against the stone floor, and the echo continues until we enter another room. A bedroom.

It looks like something from a spa. There's a king-sized four-poster bed in the center of the room with a wrought iron chandelier hanging over it that looks like it was pulled from a medieval painting. A wide archway with sliding doors leads out to the terrace.

We must be on the basement level. I wouldn't have thought there would be so much to the club, but I'm truly impressed. I smile and look at Josh.

"You like this," he states. Again, I notice the way he says things as he observes them about me.

"I do."

"But you're not sure about the Doms and subs?"

"It's different. Is that... what we'll be doing?" I look over at the bed and imagine myself tied up. Tied up and at his mercy to do with as he pleases.

I should be scared, or nervous, but... somehow, I'm not.

I'm guessing I'm on the right track when my eyes flick back up to meet his and something dark and reckless flashes in the irises of his eyes.

"Maybe... do you want to?"

I look at him and stare deeply into his eyes. I think it's safe to say that he knows I'll have a hard time telling him no. I can't remember ever saying the word in the time we've known each other.

At the same time, we haven't done anything yet that I haven't wanted to do. Everything we've been doing so far is stuff that has been pleasure for me and him.

As I continue to gaze at him, I realize that it's him. I've wanted to do all we've done because it's *him*. It's being with him, and the thrill has kept me coming back for more, wanting more, as crazy as it might be.

He told me I was his fantasy. I never realized that he was mine too.

So, why would anything else with him be anything other than pleasurable?

"Maybe..." I answer.

He pulls out my coin from his back pocket and holds it out to me.

"You're giving it back to me?" I ask, feeling my heart squeeze. Did I say the wrong thing?

"No, not the way you think. Tonight, I want to do things a little differently. Do things to your body that we haven't done yet. *Darker* things... darker things I want to do to you." His voice drops deeper, and my nerves scatter at the thought of darker things being done to me.

I only imagine what he must mean.

"So, I'm asking permission to take you over the edge, but you have to trust me with your body. You give me power to dominate you, be the master of you, own you, possess you, claim you, make you mine completely. And you will submit to me. You surrender everything to me. In return, you get ultimate pleasure. How does that sound, Giselle?"

I don't know who would say no to a reward of ultimate pleasure. It's appealing. It sounds as appealing as being given unlimited happiness. What captures me, however, is the idea of giving myself to him and being his completely. That's what tempts me.

It's the thing that entices me into the temptation of him, and it's not something I can resist.

"I want it," I say, and the lust that glitters in his eyes makes me hunger for him. "Yes, I… want you."

With his gaze hot with desire, he reaches out to run his finger along the edge of my jaw. That slight touch makes my body scream out for more, to allow him to do whatever he wants to me.

"Then your safe word is *red*."

Red…

Safe word…

Red-hot lust pulses through me, riding on the wave of forbidden pleasure.

"Say it so I know you understand me." Now he holds my face.

"Red."

"Good girl. You say that, and I stop. It all stops. Understand?"

"Yes."

CHAPTER TEN

GISELLE

"Take off the robe. Let me see you," Josh says, and I allow the robe to slide down my arms.

As the silk pools at my feet and I stand before him practically naked, it's the sexiest I've ever felt.

This negligee is the kind that was made to stay on. The see-through with the net to show off my body just the way he wants, and I'm glad he likes what he sees.

This man has seen me naked many times this week, but yet he stares at me like it's the first time. He looks me up and down, devouring me with his gaze. Then he walks around me, eyeing me up.

With the smooth edge of his forefinger, he traces a line right around me. Over the flat of my stomach, over my arms, then around to the small of my back, where he lingers, brushing over the hollow.

"From here on, Giselle, you will call me sir," he states. "And for being so truly sexy, I will reward you with one request."

A little smile slides across my mouth, but I hide it before I look back at him.

"One request?" I ask, and he dips his head to me.

"One request."

"And it can be whatever I want?"

"Yes, it can. Would you like to make your request now or later?"

I can't wait. I turn into him so I can look at him, and I want my reward now. I know what I want.

All these past days, he's called the shots and swept me off my feet and out of reality. Everything he does is so effective that it doesn't take much for him to have me practically eating out of his hands.

I want this now, before he takes control of me. That confident, sexy... daring edge of what I crave knows exactly what it wants.

"Now... I want it now," I tell him.

A wicked smile dances across his lips, and I get the feeling he knows what I'm going to ask for.

"Very well, then, you may have it now, Giselle. What would you like?"

"You," I answer, and he smooths his hand back up to cup my chin. "I want you."

"Be careful, Giselle St. John. Your eyes give you away. Be careful of what you ask for. A good girl like you shouldn't want a devil like me." He chuckles deep and low, but I see something flash in the depths of his eyes that holds my attention. It's... longing. Something more than the lust, desire, need, and want.

I see longing, like he might want me to want him too, but his warning has thrown me.

"What if I want you the same way you want me?"

"In what ways do you want me, Giselle?"

"I want to taste you, to own you... I want you to be mine completely too tonight."

The look in his eyes intensifies noticeably, and he leans closer to me. "Yes. You have me... Ladies first." He releases me and takes a step back.

Me first... oh my.

He's passed me the ball, and I get to decide what happens next. It feels like we're actually on a playground. Or in the playroom.

I step forward, closing the space between us, allowing my body and inner desires to guide me.

Tonight is about greed and lust. That means my body has to do the talking for me. The gorgeous man in front of me is what I want, and he just gave himself to me to live out the start of a fantasy that's been brewing since I first laid eyes on him.

First, I pull his shirt from the waistband of his pants and start undoing the buttons, one after the other, from top to bottom, until the soft cotton lies open on either side. Smiling to myself, I move it off down his wide powerful shoulders and push it down, watching it float over his elbows and drift down to the stone floor.

He stands there and allows me to take charge, his eyes now drinking me in with raw desire. His stare makes my nipples pebble, and I can't wait to feel his mouth on me.

I make my way down to his belt buckle and undo the belt, then the zipper on his fly. A ripple runs through me when his pants slink down his long, athletic legs, revealing the enormous bulge of his cock pressing against his Calvin Kline boxers.

He helps me out by stepping out of his shoes and socks but stops at that, leaving his boxers on, and I'm glad because he looks like a walking advert for the brand. Like he could have easily stepped off the billboard. I want to savor the look of him like this for a few seconds and seal it to my memory.

I want to remember this picture of him. Him with his cock bulging against the cotton of his boxers, erect for me.

Time for part two of this vision. A cocky grin forms on his face, accentuating the perfect angles of his jaw when I tug on the waistband of his boxers and push them down, allowing the thick length of his cock to spring free. He steps out of his boxers, and now he's naked before me.

I could see this man a million times, and still my mouth would water at the sight of him. I admit he does look better and better, but I think it's more the case of not getting enough of him.

He's standing here naked before me, and the vision is now complete. My eyes roam over his body, exploring him. From the top of his head, the masterpiece his face is, the perfection of his V-shaped torso inked with those tats and the dark happy trail that runs from his navel down to his cock. My eyes shift to his legs, lean with rippling muscles, the way you imagine on a Greek god or a Viking.

I absolutely take pleasure in the moment of walking around him too, the same way he always does me, looking over his sexy-as-fuck ass and the tattoo of a red dragon that covers his whole back.

On to the last part of my fantasy. It's not the first time I've done this, but it's the only thing I can do to him that makes me feel like I own him, like he really is mine and belongs to me.

When I make it back to his front and face him, I drop to my knees and take his cock into my hands.

His eyes rake boldly over me as I do so, roving over me with that dark desire, then molten heat as I lick over the tip of the fat head like I'm licking a lollipop.

"Are you sure that's not more for my benefit than yours?" he asks.

"No, you just get to come along for the ride," I hear myself say.

If I were by myself, I'd be jumping up and down because I definitely just scored points for being the confident, sexy, and daring woman I want to be.

The smoldering flame that enters his eyes makes me wet instantly, and I worry I may start leaking.

"Fuck," he breathes, and a proud smile pulls at the corner of my lips.

He grows harder in my hands when I run my fingers lightly over his length, which grows and fills my palms as I grip him. His thickness and perfection amaze me.

I lick him from base to tip, and his shaft strains upward in a thick curve. Pre-cum forms on the head, and I take him into my mouth, deep inside, so he can fill my mouth too. I swirl over the tip then rasp over his length in strokes that make him groan.

I start to work him, sucking hard and harder, and he laces his fingers through my hair as I bob up and down his cock.

"Fucking hell, Giselle, you're so good at this. *Fuck*," he groans, pressing me closer so I can continue to suck him.

The combo of his groans, the way he grabs my hair and my head, and what I'm doing to him, unlocks something inside me that wants to devour him. I take him deeper and suck harder.

I already know it's too much. It's too much for me too because I can already feel the tug of an orgasm, and he hasn't even touched me beyond the stroke of his finger over my skin.

It doesn't take long before he winces, and his cock pulses inside my mouth. He starts pumping, holding my head with both hands so he can fuck my face. Which just enhances the thrill racing through me.

He fucks my face, and I work him harder, coaxing his release until one last pump sends a hot spray of cum to the back of my throat. He blows into me like a hurricane, and he tastes so damn good. Like salt, man, sex, and raw, carnal desire.

I take it all in and swallow, loving the feel of the warmth that coats my mouth.

He's breathing hard and looking down at me with what can only be described as pure sinful need.

I'm breathing hard too, and my breaths come quicker as he pulls out of my mouth and clamps a hand down on my arm to pull me up.

"My turn," he informs me. That dominant voice tells me it's indeed my turn to submit and obey. Allow him to own me as he takes back control from the reward he allowed me.

CHAPTER ELEVEN

GISELLE

"Get on the bed and lie on your back," he orders, and I do.

The cool, silky sheets caress my back as I lie against them. He hovers over me, his bright baby blue's roving over me with appraisal.

"Good girl," he husks. "Remember the safe word, baby."

"I remember."

He gets onto the bed too and continues to just look at me. I always get this impression like he's committing me to memory, and it's easy to get lost in him just from that stare.

Is it wrong for me to want a man who will look at me like that forever?

Or to feel like when he does, he sees me, and it's okay to just be me? Like I'm enough.

He looked at me like that even before he knew who I was, and he never criticized.

In the lock of our gaze, my mind drifts to a place I don't want it to. To Kirk. It wasn't the fact that he called me boring that got me. It wasn't that at all. That was just the tip of the iceberg that crushed me. There was more to it than that. It was the fact that he didn't like me as a person. He didn't love me and what made me, me. None of those very basic things mattered, and yet I'm looking at Josh and seeing that those things, the things that make me who I am, are what he wants.

If only for a little while. His eyes give him away too. I don't know if he knows that.

He traces a finger over my lips and down my neck, then he lowers to press his lips to mine. *Slow and thoughtful.* That's how we kiss, as if to spark pleasure from the foundation. As he continues to kiss me in this exploratory manner, like he's tasting me, I understand that's what he's doing.

He wants me to feel everything, so he's heightening my senses to awaken the sensation I feel building in my core.

His lips leave my mouth and trace over my neck like a whisper. Warm, hot whispers caress my skin, persuading my nerve endings to spark and ignite with the heat that funnels up from my core.

He makes his way down to my breasts, kissing my nipples through the lace of the cup. As he sucks on my left breast, he parts my thighs and pushes his fingers over the already sensitive skin of my mound, then straight up into my pussy.

I gasp from the thrilling sensation and slide my leg over him so my heels can dig into his back.

My already tight nipples tighten further when he sucks harder and starts kneading and squeezing my breasts as he alternates his wild suckle.

The amplified thrill from the sensation that races through me makes my body shudder and bow to the control he has over me. Waves of overlapping pleasure hit me, curling my toes as I arch my back up into him. I moan his name over and over; it's a begging sound, and he obliges in his continued pursuit to give me pleasure. Sucking my breasts and finger-fucking me.

Eagerly and greedily, I respond to his touch, my entire body tingling. I grip his shoulders and hold on tight, but it's like I can't touch him enough or hold on tightly enough. My whole body is alive with pleasure now. It ripples and sizzles through every part of me. His gifted mouth and fingers make pleasure rocket through me, bringing me to climax.

"Josh," I cry out, and he responds by deepening the pleasure even more than it already is by moving down my body so he can replace his fingers with his tongue.

The only thing that feels better than his cock inside me is his tongue.

With a swirl, he teases and tastes the hard nub of my clit, tugging the last of the orgasm out of me, then drinking as I come.

Like always, he takes everything, and I come undone in his hands.

He stops when my breathing stills and I run a hand through his hair.

Lifting his head, he wipes his mouth with the back of his hand.

"You love that," he says, looking satisfied and proud of himself.

"Yes," I breathe.

"Yes... what?"

I right myself in my mind, knowing what he wants me to say in that instant. "Yes, sir."

It actually sounds sexy coming from me and arouses me more.

When he slides off the bed, I see he's aroused again too, already hardening up even though he finished in my mouth only minutes ago.

"Do you want more, my perfect little sub?"

"Yes, sir," I answer.

"Wonderful."

I'm glad I'm giving all the right answers. I want to see what he's going to do to me next.

He walks to the side of the bed and opens the drawer next to it. I roll my head to see when the clink of chains catches my attention.

I blink when I see he holds a set of chains attached to leather cuffs.

"Red yet, baby?" The question checks me like a checkpoint. He's making sure I want to do this.

I do, especially after the pleasure he just gave me.

"No. No, sir. I want more."

"Good girl."

He starts with my right hand. First securing the cuff to my wrist, then the chain to the loop on the headboard. It's only then that I actually realize the bed is made with the loops for the chains.

He heads to the other side and does the same thing. Last are my ankles, leaving me spread-eagled on the bed.

He's chained me up, and holy hell, do I feel at his mercy now.

I'm practically naked. His eyes drift to the crotch of the crotch-less panties, where my pussy is completely exposed, and when I move, I find I actually can't stretch my arms further than a few inches away from where I'm attached to the bed.

The next thing he does is grab a soft velvet cloth from the drawer in the nightstand and unfolds it, showing me it's a blindfold.

He gets onto the bed and smiles as he places it over my eyes first and then ties it at the back of my head.

"Listen to the sound of my voice, Giselle." He's right next to me.

"Okay, sir."

The blindfold over my eyes forces me to use my other senses. My hearing is sharper, and I hear his footsteps on the floor, then I don't hear anything for a while. I almost start to wonder if he's left me, then the clink of something else alerts me. It doesn't sound like chains, and there's a smell in the air that reminds me of that shower gel I like. The oranges. The Sanguinello oranges. That's what it smells like and ...burning. *Candles.* I don't know.

Footsteps pad near me, and then his warm breath tickles my skin.

"You will feel heat on your skin, but it will not burn you," he says. Hearing his voice after long moments without it is reassuring. I go to touch him, but the chains clink, holding me back, reminding me he's in control.

Suddenly, the heat he spoke of drops onto my chest, and I gasp. It's like a splash of desire on my already sensitive, pleasure-charged body.

Fuck, he pours a line of it down my stomach, and it feels so damn good.

"Massage wax," he breathes.

I'm smiling. "It's nice," I manage.

"It smells like you. It reminds me of you," he tells me, and I turn my head in the direction of his voice.

Before I can savor the awe I feel from his words, cold falls onto me. It's ice.

"Ohhhhh, ahhhhhhhh," I moan and arch my back. The cold and the heat together feel nice. He alternates between the two, hot and cold, hot and cold, then his lips.

His lips are hot against my skin and make me smile. They feel nice tracing down the length of my body, from the deep valley of my breasts down the flat plane of my stomach, up to my mouth, then down over my pussy lips. Josh kisses all the way down my legs and to my toes.

Then he smooths his hands right back up to my waist.

"More, baby?"

"Yes... yes sir."

He laughs. "Good girl. Let's take things up a notch."

He moves closer, and I feel the hardness of his erection press against my folds. He spreads my thighs wider to receive him, and in this position, I'm already ready to take him. I'm wet and ready, begging for his cock, begging for him to be inside me.

"Ready to go over the edge, my perfect little sub?" he asks.

"Yes, sir."

My answer makes him rub his cock against my pussy lips. Teasing me, taunting me, tempting me.

He rubs harder, then presses in but takes it away.

"Do you want my cock, little sub?" he asks, his voice now holding an air of wicked menace.

"Yes, I want your cock, sir." He brushes over my clit, sending a ripple of ecstasy through me.

"What do you want me to do to you, little sub?"

There's no thought to this. I've wanted him inside me since he pulled out of me in the early hours of the morning. I've had sex with him more times in this one week than I probably had in the whole time I was with Kirk, and I still want more.

I want more.

"Fuck me... Fuck me, sir."

"With pleasure, my little sub. Just lie back and let me fuck you."

With that, his heavy erection rubs against my slick wet opening, and he slams inside me, making my body jolt and the chains clink.

Fucking hell. As soon as he starts moving inside me, the sensation of control slips out of my grasp. Normally, I'd be holding on to him. I'd be grabbing something. Him, the sheets, or whatever I can get my hands on.

But I can't. There's nothing but air, and I can't see him. All I can do is feel him.

I feel him inside me, his hands on my waist and then my hips as he grips harder and starts thrusting deep, then fucking me hard.

Stars speckle my vision against the blackness of the cloth, and sounds of raw ecstasy and pleasure fill the room, along with the echo of our bodies slapping together.

Wave after wave of pleasure hits me the more he gives me exactly what he promised. *Ultimate pleasure.*

I come on that thought, and the tension rises again, coiling from where it previously emerged.

"Ahhhh... Joshhhhh!!" I moan and arch into him.

"That's right, baby, say my name. Scream it. Fucking scream it," he commands, and I scream.

I scream and go wild, grinding against him as he continues to fuck me. It's the two of us now as I fuck him too. He holds me in place and stops to allow me to move against him.

I come again from the wildness that splinters me in two, severing me from this plane of existence as more pleasure comes for me.

He, however, is still rock hard inside me.

Surprise fills me when he pulls out as we're moving, and I feel lost, like heat has left my body. He undoes the chains from my wrists and ankles, and being able to move again feels weird.

That feels weird, but then he picks me up and sets me down on him. Chains clink again, and one is attached to my right wrist and something else.

He takes the blindfold off me, and when my eyes adjust, I see he's handcuffed me to him.

"You said something about owning me too." He smirks.

"Oh my God," I breathe.

"You can thank God later and give my regards once I'm done with you."

His overconfidence is through-the-roof sexy.

He raises the hand that's cuffed to me and plants it behind his head so I'm forced to lean forward with my breasts in his face.

I settle down on his cock, and he smiles when I moan.

With his free hand, he takes the edge of my waist.

"Ride me, baby, fuck me in whatever way you wish, little sub."

"Yes... sir." I just manage to get that out. I think this is it for me. The pleasure is too much. He's too much.

His massive cock inside me is too much. It's searing into me like a furnace in my loins. Once again, he fills me up, stripping everything away from me but my need for him.

I move against him, bouncing up and down on his cock, my breasts bouncing in his face.

With our faces close, hands locked, we move together in a raw scandalous rhythm. He holds me tightly in place as he rams into me, but I take him and take what he gives me, giving back as much as he gives me.

He growls as his cock pulses inside me and flips me over onto my back, then whips me around so that my back is pressed against his chest with our hands still locked together.

I'm in the lock of another orgasm. Right there at the edge from all we've done tonight, however, what he does next pushes me that much more, and I gasp. With his left hand, he presses into the tight rosette of my asshole.

"I want you here. I want you here, baby. Has anybody ever been there before?"

"No... Nobody has." My breath hitches as I think of what it will feel like.

"Will you let me?" he asks, and the gentle caress of his words strokes my heart. He doesn't know he's the second man I've ever been with. He won't know that the buzz of wildness that's taking me makes me wish he was the last. *My only.*

I'm crossing a line I shouldn't cross. The lines of this little arrangement already feel blurred, and I'm agreeing to more.

"Yes," I say.

"Good girl. Just trust me."

I do.

He bends me over, takes hold of his cock, and presses the head against my ass. My lips part when he eases in. This feels so different, so new, but so right.

I gasp when he makes his way into me and starts moving.

This feels too good. His cock pulsing in my asshole feels unbelievably good, and I can't believe I'm this kinky.

He speeds up, and a white wall of rippling fire flashes through me. I close my eyes, and everything explodes, consuming me whole. The bone-tingling orgasm he sends through my body shatters my soul and reverberates through every part of my body.

With my heart pounding and body quivering, I see stars and feel fire. It drains me, but the tension of his cock throbbing inside me as he thunders into me, filling me up again with his hot virile cum, gives me the strength to cry out one last time with him as we fall right over the edge together.

I fall and take him, but he holds me and cushions me, anchoring me against the blow.

All I feel is pleasure.

I know, though, that I'm in trouble when the thought hits me that I'll only ever feel like this with him.

CHAPTER TWELVE

JOSH

Dad's talking, but all I can think about is her.

Giselle St. John.

The woman I wasn't supposed to sleep with.

The woman Dad thinks I'm not sleeping with. He thinks I've trained her really well, and he's proud of me.

We're in his office, and he's been talking to me for the last half hour. All I've heard out of his praise, though, was a handful of words, because fuck damn, am I caught in my own game.

I want to say it started that night when she said she wanted me, but I think it was before. That was just the making of what was going to happen. Her telling me that was what cemented it.

She asked me if I got to be hers too when I first presented her with the offer, and it threw me off kilter.

What knocked me off my damn perch of control, though, was that first night. The first time I laid eyes on her at the club.

I looked at her, and the whole place froze. Everything froze. Now I have that moment and everything else about her playing over and over in my head.

I see it and hear her telling me she wants me.

She's not the first woman to want me. No, it's not that. What it is, is she's the first woman to ask for me. To desire me for more than the money and my looks.

More than power.

I've been like this for the last two months, very aware that I just have one more month with her before our little arrangement of fun is supposed to end.

"Joshua." Dad says my name with more insistence. It pulls me right out of my thoughts.

"I'm sorry, what did you say? I was thinking about that last thing you said." I didn't hear shit. I have no idea what he's been talking about for the last five minutes. I said thanks when he told me he was proud, and I said yes when he asked if it was Giselle who took the lead on the last few cases.

He chuckles and sits forward. "You're miles away, my boy. I was asking you if you thought that maybe she might be ready to do some work on her own, with mild supervision. I think she'll be great here once you switch over to the other building."

This time, I'm paying attention. I'm damn well paying attention. He said when I switch over to the other building, like he's made up his mind already. That sounded positive and reminds me of the first thing I wanted. My goals for my future, my career.

"She's a brilliant attorney with a passion for her work. We have a real asset in her. She's worked on the cases with heart," I answer, purposely not mentioning the other building. Dad couldn't look prouder.

"I see that. I do. That was especially why I wanted you to take care with her. I really wanted to train her myself, but duty called. I read her files and saw that she'd been through quite a bit in the last year. Her father's death, and while the files never mentioned this, and I definitely don't tend to get involved in celeb gossip, I know she was with Kirk Ryan for years, and he didn't seem to treat her right."

I narrow my eyes at him. This is the first I'm hearing this. I'm not into football like Dad, but I know who Kirk Ryan is.

That guy is a prick and a half. One of our attorneys worked for him on a defamation lawsuit a few months back where he was suing some tabloid for publishing him having a threesome with a bunch of models at a Christmas party.

Okay... maybe I'm no better when it comes to scandals, but that guy is the kind that is a straight-up asshole with no regard for anything.

"She was with him?" I ask with narrowed eyes.

"Yeah, I know. Definitely not the type of guy I would imagine her with. They dated in college and broke up eight months ago."

I hold my tongue. Christmas was nine months ago, so he was with her when that story came out. Geez. He cheated on her big time. *Did she know?*

I really hope it was her who broke up with him and not the other way around. Something deep down tells me it's not. I think it was him who ended it.

She dated him in college... I bet she never thought he'd turn into an asshole. I can't imagine he was the way he was now when she met him. Then again, she's with me.

I'm not like him though. I don't cheat, and there's no way I'd cheat on her if she really was mine like that.

I'd keep her.

Shit... What the fuck?

What am I thinking? This thing I have with her is fun.

This arrangement we have, me and her, is about fun. We literally come from two different worlds. One where I know we wouldn't collide even if the earth shifted and made her bump into me.

That first night we met, she was at the club with friends. My observance told me they'd been there before. The club was their thing, and it was her first time. Had she not gone, we wouldn't have met that way.

"Well," Dad says, "I guess now that you have some background and context, you know why I was the way I was. She is talented, and I'd like to keep her. Joshua, you have a rep I don't like. I won't lie to you and tell you that I enjoy hearing about this woman and that woman you slept with, and in the office too."

I groan inwardly. *Fucking hell.* "Dad, I've changed," I remind him for the millionth time.

"I definitely agree, and I can see that you are trying. That's the part I like."

"Enough so I can be at the other building?" I ease the conversation back to that.

I want this promotion and the chance to be my own boss. Being in control of the other building is essentially him giving it to me. I'm more than ready to take charge. I am.

When he nods, I can't help but smile.

"Yes... but please don't get too excited yet. Joshua, you are my son, and it's been hard trying to separate myself from being your boss and the parent who wants to give you everything."

"Dad, I have worked hard here. Even when I was an asshole who, yeah, I admit that I was the office flirt, and I did sleep around. But I know you... father or not, you wouldn't have stood for my bullshit if I wasn't good."

He looks at me. I'm right. I know I am.

"I agree. Let's just see how the next month goes. It's fair to continue the tasks I set out for you and Riley. He's doing well too on his front."

"Okay," I say, agreeing because I have to.

He's boss. If I want what I want, I have to play by the rules.

He nods, and I stand up.

"I'll see you later," I tell him.

"You know, we're having dinner with Jennifer and her family Sunday, if you want to join us." He looks hopeful.

"No, thank you." Before I met Giselle, I would have allowed him to continue this shit with Jennifer, but before Giselle, I didn't have better, and I feel like I'm somewhat inclined to let him know that I've been with a woman who is good and decent. Since I can't outrightly tell him that, I do the next best thing. "Dad, you may want to get your head out of the clouds when it comes to Jennifer. She's not the person you think she is, and when I do decide to get married, it will be for love. A woman I love the way you love Mom. It won't be with someone you've picked for me."

I know I shocked him to shit because I don't talk like that. I've left him speechless, staring after me as I walk out the door.

I head to the break room, and I'm glad when I see Matt inside. He smiles when he sees me.

My friend has upgraded himself from playboy to boyfriend. He's now dating Elena, and being her boyfriend looks good on him. He looks happy.

"Bro, how did it go?" he asks me. "Did your old man grill you again?"

I chuckle. "Not so much. I'd say the meeting went well."

Matt nods with approval. "Great, we should go out later for a drink."

"I can't." It's the same answer I've been giving him for the last couple of months when he asks to meet up later in the evening. We've gone for lunch together, but I spend my evenings with Giselle.

"Tomorrow, then? Friday night wildness on the town, you and me."

"I'm seeing Giselle tomorrow night too."

He frowns. "And every night in between." Now he laughs at me and shakes his head. "Don't you see what's happening here?"

I raise my brows. "What?"

"Josh, when was the last night that didn't involve you and Giselle in some sexual encounter, *and* at The Dark Odyssey?"

I don't have to think. We've been there practically every night for the last two months.

It was just a handful of nights that we didn't spend together, but we more than made up for it.

"I can't think."

"And you're okay with that, being in this arrangement where you just have fun. A game at the club?"

This guy always knows how to push my buttons and get me thinking.

The truth is, I do want more from her. I always want more, and I'm here trying to stop myself from moving past boundaries I set up.

I want to see her outside of the club and know that side of her too. I want the whole package.

"It's not just a game anymore, is it?" he asks.

"What game?" comes the most irritating voice I've ever heard in my life.

Riley walks through the door with his pompous ass.

I hate that except the difference in eye color, he looks a lot like me. He has dark brown eyes, and mine are bright blue. Other than that, we could be brothers for the similarities between us. Right from height to fucking shoe size.

He's five years older than me and has always thought that meant he had some power over me. The prick is doing it now as we stand here.

"Is there a game?" he asks. "I wasn't aware of one, unless you mean this foolish competition between us that I will clearly win."

Fucking asshole. I smile at him, but I'm balling my fists at my sides. "Why don't you go fuck yourself, man?" I counter.

I absolutely hate his guts. We've always been at each other's throats right from when we were kids.

The thing he hates about me is that I have parents who love each other. His got divorced when he was twelve. Uncle Jackson likes to think he's some kind of king, but he's another prick I can't stand. My parents will never tell me this, but that divorce was down to cheating. His father cheated on his mother, and Riley's had four stepmothers since.

He can't stand the stability I have in my life and that my ass didn't use the silver spoon I was born with the way he does.

"I don't need to do things like that, Josh. Not when your little associate looks so damn scrumptious. I'm very aware you can't sleep with her. That doesn't mean I can't." He laughs. "I'll bet her pussy is as good as—"

Motherfucker, he doesn't get to finish.

I land a fist straight in his face so hard it knocks him to the ground.

The prick gets up, ready, and launches at me, coming after me like when we were kids. We aren't kids anymore though. I'm not the scrawny boy he used to push around.

I have muscle on him, and I'm already hyped up on the fact that this fucking competition exists. He's not taking my girl.

A one-two punch sends him back to the floor. Matt grabs me, holding me back to stop me from beating Riley's ass senseless, and just then, Giselle walks in, looking bewildered. I see her and see the knowing look that enters his eyes. He knows she means more to me than what everyone else can see. But he also knows to beware of me.

I shrug Matt's arms off me and straighten up.

"You," I say, pointing to Riley. Blood has started to pour from his nose. "You stay the fuck away from her. Don't push me or think you can test me. Blood won't matter if you do."

At that moment, I don't care who's watching me. I take Giselle's hand and lead her away.

I lead her back to my office, again not caring about the looks people cast my way. I know people talk here. I know people talk to Dad. That's how he found out about the temps and any other shit he might have found out about me.

If someone wants to be a prick and tell him they saw me holding Giselle's hand, I'll find a way to deal with it. Right now, the possessive side of me that truly believes she's mine is acting out, acting like she is mine. It won't allow me to hear another man talk about my woman that way. And it won't allow me to let her go.

I'm still holding her hand even when we walk inside and close the door, shutting out Sheila's stares as she breaks her neck to see what's going on. She'd better not mess with me either. I upgraded her from receptionist to secretary because she's reliable, and I also practically tripled her salary.

I pray it's not her who fills Dad's ears with updates on my extra-curricular activities.

A little squeeze to my hand snaps my attention back to reality. Giselle runs her finger over the top of my thumb, and a blush creeps into her cheeks.

"Josh, are you okay?" she asks. She's going to have more questions than that. She heard me say enough to know I was fighting over a woman.

My threats to Riley were enough to tell all. I didn't even look back at Matt, who must have been shocked to shit by my actions.

Fuck, I got so mad at Riley, it completely escaped me that he knew I wasn't supposed to sleep with Giselle. That meant he and Dad were talking, and I fucking hate when that happens. Riley acts like he's a saint when he's not. He acts like he's so much better than me so he can kiss ass and fucking brownnose to get ahead of me because he's jealous.

"Yes, fine," I tell her.

She glances down at my hand still holding hers. "We're holding hands in front of people, and you were fighting with your cousin... *and* you threatened him."

I bite down hard on my back teeth and look at her. As I do, I find that I can't look away.

We're holding hands at the office, and I've been sneaking around with her for the last two months. This is not the kind of woman you sneak around with.

Look at her... *beautiful and perfect*. Inside and out. She's the kind of woman you show off.

She's the kind of woman you make sure people know is yours. She's the kind of woman I would make sure people knew was mine. Riley wouldn't have been idiot enough to taunt me the way he did just now if he knew she was mine.

I sigh and release her hand on that thought.

Fuck... what the fuck?

I need a drink or something. I walk over to the window and gaze out at the lake in the distance. It serves as a distraction.

What soothes me more is the dainty hand on my arm. I turn

back to face Giselle, and I think about it all. What if I changed the rules of the game?

What if I did that?

I don't know how to be the kind of man she deserves, but surely, I can do better than that idiot Kirk.

"Josh, who were you talking about? It sounded serious, and I've never seen you get so mad. Did he say something about someone... a woman of sorts?"

Shit, I just realize the other thing she could be thinking, that I was fighting with my cousin over some woman indeed, but not her. Considering I'm the watcher, the observer, I should have picked up on that straight away.

"It was you," I answer, and her eyes widen.

"What?"

"Don't worry about it. Just don't talk to him. He's an ass."

She smiles a little. "Josh, you call everybody an ass. If they wear the wrong color or eat the wrong food, they're an ass."

I chuckle. "Okay, maybe I was having off days when I called those people whatever the shit I called them. Him though... it's real."

The seriousness returns to her face. "What did he say about me?"

I cup her face. "Baby, please... don't worry about it."

The longer I look at her, the more I contemplate the question looming over my mind, and I decide that I can try.

I have a month left with her. It could be a month of something else too for me. Something different.

That means I have to be the one to change things up.

"Giselle, how about we do something different tomorrow night?" I ask. It's going to take planning.

"Different?" A saucy glint sparks her eyes. "What more different can we do?"

I can think of a few things at The Dark Odyssey I want to try with her. That's the beauty of it. The place is filled with everything to live out your wildest fantasies. Even when you do it, it's guaranteed that the next time you try, it will be different.

It's just like her. She is my wild fantasy, and I can't get enough.

I want more.

"There's a lot, baby, but this will be different. You'll like it."

"Will I?"

I nod. She will. It'll be something from her world. We are from two different worlds. There really was no way that we would have gotten involved had she not gone to the club that night, but she did.

She entered my world. Now I'm going to cross over to hers.

"Come here," I say, beckoning her to my lips for a kiss I savor, the way I savor her.

CHAPTER THIRTEEN

GISELLE

Rachel and Jia are smiling at me.

They lean over the table at the coffeehouse as they're listening to me babble on about Josh.

I'm listening to myself too. They're intrigued and hanging on to every word I say.

I feel like I'm talking, and I know it's me who's talking, but it doesn't feel like me. Months ago, when I first felt the signs of me slipping over this invisible line of fun with Josh, I reined myself in and tried to focus.

Focus on my job and focus on controlling my emotions. The thing I learned about emotions is that it gets to a point where you can't keep them on a leash. You can only restrain them for so long, but your true feelings come out eventually. Mine did yesterday, and now I'm eager to see what Josh has planned for later.

"Giselle," Jia begins with a bright smile on her face, "I'm gonna say that I love this. I really do. You've changed. You've become this woman who is willing to push the limits. It's a good thing."

Rachel nods her agreement and raises her coffee cup like she would a wine glass.

"Hear! Hear! I agree, and I'm proud," Rachel says. Her eyes twinkle with delight.

It's nice to see my friends happy for me, even if there actually is nothing concrete to tell them. I'm just excited about later, and that feels nice. It feels good. It means I'm healing. It means I moved on from Kirk and he doesn't affect me anymore.

"So, any idea at all what you guys will be doing tonight?" Rachel asks.

I shake my head. "No. I have no clue. He didn't tell me what to wear, so I'm at a loss. He said to meet him in the park by the lake at eight. And as per usual, he told me to go home early."

They look at each other and smile.

"I can't figure it out," Jia states. "Maybe he's thinking of some new ways to have sex or prep you for your club spree later."

They both start to giggle. I thought that too and decided I wouldn't hurt my brain trying to guess. I'm going to wear something nice. A little skater dress that's smart casual. That should work since when we go to the club, we always end up naked in either the suite or the playroom. I christened that room after he first took me over the edge in the playroom because that's what it felt like to me. A place for us to play around with each other with fantasy adult toys, and my, have we surely played. That man has done everything to me. Things I would never even dream of or know were possible.

More significant than that is how I feel when I'm with him. He's the fantasy and the man whom I trust to take me on whatever wild adventure he conjures up.

Jia straightens as an idea seems to have hit her. "What if it's dinner?"

I smile at the thought of that. "Dinner?"

"He said the river, right? There are some beautiful riverside restaurants. It's gonna be something like that. I bet it is."

"That means outside the club," Rachel adds and wiggles her brows.

My breath stills. The thought of Josh wanting to see me outside the club and work is unreal.

We went to the club last night, and he seemed different. More attentive. It was the first night when it wasn't just about sex. We talked more. I remember talking before I fell asleep. Usually, I'd get lost with him inside me and wake up like it too.

This morning when I woke up in his arms, he held me there for a little longer.

Jesus... am I allowing myself to get in over my head with this man?

"Outside the club would be nice. I won't start thinking up stuff though. I shouldn't," I state. It's time for that reality check. I shouldn't jump from A to Z, open my mind to new possibilities, because then it will be my fault when it doesn't happen.

I do wonder though... if maybe it could be more.

That fight he had with Riley said a lot. He hit his cousin because Riley said something about me. Something Josh didn't like. It must have been pretty bad for him to act that way and then threaten him.

I didn't know what was said, but when I realized the fight was about me, something unlocked inside me that believed I belonged to him. The way he looked at me and held my hand is something I'll remember forever. No matter what.

Rachel reaches across the table and taps the top of my hand. A smile fills her face.

"Open mind, Giselle. It means there's no harm hoping for stuff with a guy you clearly like. The openness of your mind allows you to think of all possibilities. It means if one thing doesn't happen, then something else might. Since Josh seems to be really into you, I doubt you'll be disappointed either way."

It's times like these when I'm grateful for my friendship with her. Jia nods, agreeing with that. Me too.

I started to change my way of thinking when I embraced the possibility of an open mind.

Rachel's about to continue but stops when she lifts her head and looks over my shoulder. A little breath falls from her lips, then the widest smile spreads over her face.

I follow her gaze and see Dante walking through the door of the coffeehouse.

And damn, the man looks even better than the last time we saw him.

He has that sexy tough guy presence, like someone like Hugh Jackman, but Dante Lombroso is Italian and is an Italian stallion in every essence of the word. His dark hair is cut into a neat faux hawk, and he has the kind of face to turn heads. We aren't the only ones looking at him. That man will get to a hundred and still be gorgeous. Even then I wouldn't blame Rachel for her obsession with him, and I don't blame her now as she practically flies over to him, her movement one fluid motion. Realization hitting it was him then flying into his arms.

Jia and I look at each other. Jia sips her coffee, blushing. She never blushes, ever. I just keep quiet and look back at the two. Rachel with her dad's best friend.

I look and try to do that thing Josh does. *Watch. Observe.*

Observe and try to see if there is more to the way Dante looks at Rachel than he always has before.

They're only paces away from us, so I can just make out what they're saying.

"My God, look at you," he says, fussing over her. I don't miss the twinkle in his eyes as he takes Rachel's shoulders. "You look fantastic, Princesca."

He's looking at her like they haven't seen each other in years, but it was just roughly over ten months ago. Just before Kirk and I broke up.

Princesca... I love the endearment. I have always loved it, and as for Rachel, it really makes her head swell.

"Thank you, so do you," Rachel replies. "When did you get back? I thought you were coming back next month."

"Oh... I had some stuff to look into. Best to come home early." He nods. "I'm just here for the week."

"Oh, will I get to see you again?" Rachel asks. I feel sorry for her. She was crushed when he moved away.

"Of course, I'm not going to come home and not see my favorite girl. Let's do dinner. You and me. And we can get ice cream."

The dinner part of that suggestion was nice. I almost thought it was on the right track, but ice cream... She told me he'd take her for ice cream at the kiddie parlor, just like he did when she was five.

"Sure, okay. That sounds great," Rachel answers, and I'm crushed for her when a woman with platinum blond hair walks in looking like she just stepped off the runway and stops at Dante's side.

I feel even worse when Dante's face lights up when he sees her. He releases Rachel and slips his arm around the woman who gives Rachel a stiff smile.

"Rachel, this is Maria, my fiancée. I'm so glad you got to meet her," Dante says.

That's when I stop observing. I stop listening then too and turn back to Jia. I don't need to watch anymore. Jia looks the same as me—crestfallen. She shakes her head and bites the inside of her lip.

Moments later, when Rachel returns to us, her skin looks pale and her eyes too wide, like they're tired from upholding the façade of her looking excited.

She sits and stares openly ahead of us. It's my hand on her elbow that brings her out of the trance.

"What's wrong with me? I'm so crazy," she says, and I feel worse when a tear runs down her cheek. Jia reaches for her other hand.

"I think it's time to move on," Jia states, and Rachel nods.

"Well, she seems nice, right? If I love him, then I should be happy that he's with someone nice." She looks at me as if for strength, and I freeze because she's shocked me.

She's never said she loved him. Not out loud, although it wasn't exactly hard to guess.

"Yes," I answer. It seems like the best thing to say because what else is there? Dante's getting married. We just saw his fiancée, and while she didn't look all that thrilled to meet Rachel, it doesn't mean she and Dante aren't meant to be with each other. Honestly, I might not be too thrilled either if my fiancé was holding Rachel the way Dante was, no matter the innocence in it. The woman looked like she just stepped off the runway, but Rachel looks like she could be walking right next to her on it. The threat of another beautiful woman was the reason why Maria looked at her the way she did.

"I'm sorry, Rachel," I add, and she nods. The light returns to her eyes.

"It's okay." She smiles, but I can see it's a smile she doesn't feel. "I'm fine. I was just thrown seeing him, that's all. And meeting her for real. Don't let me ruin your excitement for later. I think you will be quite surprised and happy with whatever Josh has planned."

"You think so?" I ask, going with the subject shift, although I can see she's not as okay as she's saying. I just hope that she'll talk to me when she needs to.

"Yes, I absolutely do. I think we should go shopping for makeup or something, to highlight the difference."

I laugh and decide to humor her, and myself too.

I ended up buying a dress. It's nothing fancy. Just a little black dress with a lace top that I'm wearing under a beige blazer. It floats about my legs as I walk down the path to the riverside. In my mind, I'm thinking that Josh might have chosen a restaurant. Nerves made me eat more than usual, though, so I'm not actually hungry.

I see him just across the way, near the park entrance. He's not wearing his usual suave clothes that he normally wears when we meet at the club. He's wearing a leather biker jacket and dark jeans hung low on his hips. This is the first I've seen him in casual wear, and he looks even better. This matches the bad-boy version of him he portrays to the world.

Before him is a whole host of cars where people have gathered. I didn't know there was anything going on tonight. Usually, I'm clued up on anything like that.

He sees me, and I rush over to him, straight into his arms, my lips to his. I can't believe this is me.

Me and him kissing under the moonlight. It feels like a different version of us. One that I could easily get lost in forever.

He pulls out of the kiss slowly and catches my face, beaming down at me.

"Woman, you're going to get me in trouble," he says with a wolfish grin.

"What kind of trouble?"

He looms before me and nibbles on my bottom lip. "Indecent exposure, having sex right here with you dressed like that," he answers, and I giggle when he reaches down to catch the hem of my dress.

Thank God he doesn't pull it all the way up like he would if we were at the club. He does look at my panties, though, and nods.

"Yes, I'm keeping those tonight," he says, and I laugh.

"Josh, if you take any more of my panties, I won't have any left." I can't get over how he is. Every time I change some fragrance about me, he takes my underwear, bras, and panties. Anything that smells like me. "What will you do then?"

"Like fuck. What the hell kind of question is that? I will just keep you," he replies, like that's the obvious answer. It makes me wish for it, even though I shouldn't. I know it's just a matter of speech.

Him keeping me, however, is a thought to relish.

"Can I have you, Miss St. John?" he asks, enhancing the wild, sexy vision that enters my mind.

"Yes, you may, sir," I tease.

"Jesus... don't you dare. Tonight is different."

"So I see. We're in a park with cars. Is there another sex club nearby?"

"No... there isn't."

I'm not sure that what I'm seeing is right, but he looks kind of nervous.

"What are we doing tonight?"

"This," he answers, taking my hand.

I glance up at him and smile as he leads me closer to the cars. We walk down past a station wagon with a couple sitting on the hood. Looking around, I see people either gathered on blankets or sitting on the tops of their cars.

It's eight o'clock at night, and people are gathered like they're here for some kind of concert.

We stop by a Porsche, and Josh points way ahead of us as a set of bright lights turn on, illuminating the men who are setting up a screen.

It's a cinema-sized screen, and I realize what we're doing, why we're here.

"The cinema?" I ask, looking back at Josh.

"Yeah. Thought you might like this."

I love it. "I've never been to an open-air cinema before."

"Me neither." He beams, and I laugh when he picks me up and sets me on top of the car.

Josh normally drives a convertible. I've never seen him with this car before.

He reaches into the car and grabs a massive bag of popcorn, hands it to me, and gets on top of the car to sit next to me. I look at him, wondering what this is.

As the film starts, my heart stills in my chest when I see *Casablanca* come on the screen.

I look from the screen to Josh in complete disbelief.

This is so much more than thinking we were going to a restaurant. This is so much more than anyone has ever done for me. It's so much more than what I expected from us.

He kisses the top of my nose and smiles. "I watch, remember? You really like this," he whispers.

"I really do."

"So, I want to like it as well," he says and slips his arm around me.

I rest my head against his chest and allow my mind to drift and slip into another fantasy. This moment and this feeling that settles over me.

Happiness.

CHAPTER FOURTEEN

GISELLE

Happiness...

It continued through the film, and now that it's over I don't know what we'll do.

We're normally at The Dark Odyssey. We're normally in a bed. We would have normally had sex several times by now and played around with each other.

But... we're here in a normal setting, and we've arrived at the part of the evening when I'm supposed to go home.

This was a date, and it was a nice date.

What next, though?

As the credits move across the screen and people start packing up, Josh slides off the car and makes his way around to me to lift me down.

He kisses me the minute my feet touch the ground, and the kiss consumes me. Before it can turn hungry, though, he moves away, but not too far.

"Come home with me," he says.

"What?" I ask in disbelief.

"Giselle, I'd like you to come home with me. If it's not too...

weird. I know that tonight was different, and I probably should have asked you out, but I didn't want to ruin the surprise of it."

"It was amazing. I loved every minute of it."

"Good, and *Casablanca* is my new favorite film," he adds.

"You didn't think it was boring?"

He narrows his eyes at me. "You know me well enough by now to know I'll tell you exactly what I think."

I smile at that with appreciation. "I want to go home with you."

"You sure?"

I nod.

He doesn't need to be told twice. He just opens the door for me to get in the car.

———

His house looks exactly like the kind I imagined him in.

Something massive and dominant that would take up a whole block.

So, when the wide gates open to allow his car to head up a driveway that took us a few minutes to drive up, I wasn't surprised. Nor was I surprised to see the mansion rising into my view with a picturesque vision of the lake behind it and what I can make out to be a sailboat off in the distance.

Okay... so maybe I didn't imagine all this. I just knew his home would be big and my little apartment would be no match for it.

I'm also not shocked when we go inside and encounter a maid who looks like she was just finishing up for the day.

She looks surprised to see Josh and shocked to see me.

I get that she could be surprised to see him because we're always away at the club, and I know for sure he hasn't been home most Friday nights as they've been spent with me.

The shock of seeing me, though, is something else.

"Joshua, I wasn't expecting you," she beams. There's a slight accent to her voice. It sounds French.

"I know," Josh says. "Juliana, this is Giselle."

"Hello, Giselle," Juliana states with a wide smile.

"Hi, it's nice to meet you," I say to her.

"Likewise. Well, I better be going. I'll see you sometime Monday." She nods and leaves us.

Josh nods and waits about two seconds after she walks through the door before he grabs me and hoists me over his shoulder caveman style.

I'm laughing so much I can barely contain myself. He flips my dress up and runs a firm hand over my ass.

"Finally, I get to have you all to myself. In my bed," he booms, giving my ass a good squeeze.

We enter his room, which looks a little like our playroom at the club. It's medieval looking with the same wrought iron fixtures. I realize then that's his thing.

I like it. He sets me down on the bed, and it takes a handful of seconds before we're naked and tangled with each other. Naked and kissing, his hands touching me everywhere while I touch him too.

Everything we've done over the last two days has felt more sensual. It's been fast-paced and seems deeper than before. Like someone turned up the speed we were traveling on the rollercoaster of this wild romance.

The minute his cock sears into me, something happens inside me that feels like so much more. A blast of energy sweeps through me, severing me from everything that isn't him.

It burns and scorches, yet it sends a shiver through me of hot and cold. Just like the wax and the ice. Hot and cold and pleasure.

Him... it's all him, and I'm trying so hard to stay on this side of the line. I could be looking at it before me. In my mind's eye, I'm watching myself on a road, and the line is painted right there in front of me. Telling me this is the limit I should keep within.

I know the line is there and I shouldn't cross it, but my feet have kept moving, trying to move me over it every time my feelings grow for Josh.

Tonight, though, the line is blurring. It blurs, then fades, then disappears like someone erased it as we come together in a shared release as he laces his fingers through mine. His face is pressed against mine, and our lips are touching. He's holding my hand, holding me. Being this close to him, I can see the unmistakable look in his eyes that's a tell of the change I feel.

He feels it too. I can see it.

That change and the energy that pulsed over us was us making love. It didn't feel like sex. It was different, as different as we are.

"More... I want that again," he mutters.

"Me too."

My answer feels like something more too. Just like his request. I stay the night, then I stay the weekend. The next week passes, and we're either at his place or mine. We bounce in and out of each other's world's, from home to home, work, and then the club. We play at the club, and then we watch my old films at my place.

We go sailing. I learn so much more about him, and he learns about me.

More.

It's all more. I find myself telling him about Kirk, and he listens. He listens to me, and I listen to him.

We exist outside time and space. We just are.

Three weeks later sees us at the club, and we become the couple I saw that first night entering the exhibitionist box.

We become them, and I live that first fantasy I conjured up with him.

Me and him inside the box, devouring each other, naked and free and wild and reckless, sharing raw erotic pleasure at its finest.

I will never forget the experience of being with him like that or the way I have been when I've been with him.

It's Monday morning again, and so much time has passed. I haven't been unaware of it, nor the fact that this is my last week with Josh.

This is it, and I don't know what will happen.

He'll be moving to the new building, and he'll have new staff. I won't see him every day the way I have been, and I don't know if I'll see him otherwise because I'm not sure what we are.

I got here early today and prepped for one of my cases. I have a client who has a trademark dispute, and I wanted to read through the files a little more. There's some information I needed in the archives, so I thought it would be a good distraction to go and check it out.

I was right. I've been in there for at least an hour before I start thinking about Josh, and I'm only pulled from my work because he sends me a message asking to meet for coffee. It's then too that I see how early it still is.

It's just gone nine, so Josh would have only just gotten in.

I text back letting him know I'll meet him at the coffee shop in ten minutes, but footsteps make me look up.

The sound breaks through the silence, and seeing Riley walking toward me sends a shiver down my spine.

Josh might be judgmental, and he might sometimes show too much animosity, but he's not wrong to do so when it comes to his cousin.

Riley really is an ass, and I've noticed that the man has made it a point since the day of the fight to look at me more intensely every time he sees me. I start to gather my things so he doesn't get any ideas to talk to me for longer than necessary, but he walks right up to me.

"Rushing away so soon?" he says, looking me over. His gaze lands on my breasts and lingers there for longer than I like.

"I'm really busy today," I answer, not wanting to be rude. It's hard, though, when he's still looking at my breasts. "My eyes are up here," I say with an edge to my voice that makes him look up.

"I'm very aware of where your eyes are. I doubt it's where your brain is though. Any woman with half a brain can see that my cousin is a playboy. Is that what you're into?"

I'm not sure what I should say here.

The bottom line is, I've been sleeping with my boss. There's no policy on office relationships being forbidden, but it's stricter when it comes to direct line management. Even without that stipulation, though, I know I'm not supposed to be sleeping with my boss, and I know not to confirm that I am to his cousin.

"I don't think that's any of your business," I answer.

He laughs. "So, you're not denying it, then? You're seeing him, fucking him. Did he promise you a sure sign off if you did? Or maybe he paid you to be his personal slut."

My cheeks heat up at the same time my blood boils. "Excuse me?"

"Oh, please, don't act so innocent. I know you aren't as stupid as you look or appear to be. You must know what the man is like, and his... unconventional habits. Whores in his bed, a prostitute here and there. Personal waitresses from The fucking Dark Odyssey you can hire to do whatever the fuck you want. Of course, I would ask you that."

Oh my God... He wouldn't be saying all of that if it weren't true. The mention of The Dark Odyssey snaps me.

"He wasn't supposed to get involved with you, but Josh is like that. He defies authority."

"What are you talking about?"

"Because your boyfriend is such a playboy, his father laid down the law. We're in competition for management of the new branch. My tasks was to restructure the training program for the interns. His tasks was not to sleep with you or sleep around. That's the kind of man you are with. That's the man who will be in charge of something I should manage. The kind who gives his family's company a bad name." He takes a breath and shakes his head. I hate that he looks so much like Josh. The two are not alike, but the similarities strike me at this moment because it's like the words are coming from Josh. "He goes from one woman to the next. You'll just be pussy to him come next week, and you're here keeping up this façade with him as his whore while his father thinks he's been the perfect saint."

I can't believe what I'm hearing. But why am I surprised? He's right. I'm not stupid. I should know all this.

I should know because Josh met me at The Dark Odyssey. Should I kid myself into thinking he was just there for the night simply exploring the place?

The private lounge he has and the access to a bedroom and the playroom and everywhere else is all at his fingertips because he uses them.

He's used them, and he didn't start when he met me.

He's well versed in all kinds of things, and I've just been on this wild ride with him.

Riley laughs when he sees he's thrown me and managed to faze me.

"Awww, there, there, I really hope you weren't fool enough to fall for him. Guess what, though, there's light at the end of the tunnel. When he casts you aside, I'll be here. I wouldn't mind testing out that body of yours since you're putting out. I'm sure I pay more than him."

"You asshole," I snap and step back when he steps forward.

"Watch it, girlie, I'm a senior partner here. Doesn't matter whose cock your riding. One word from me, and you're done. I fucking mean it."

I can see he does.

I can absolutely see that he means every word he's saying and relishing the threat he's handing me, probably because of the way Josh handled him last time.

The door opens, and Sheila comes in smiling with her usual brightness. I'm relieved to see her and for the chance to escape.

I don't look at Riley as I rush away. I don't look at anyone. I rush to my office and put my head down on the desk, trying to steady my nerves and my racing heart.

I'm thinking, and maybe thinking clearly for the first time.

This thing with Josh was fun, and I hate to admit this, but I was stupid enough to fall for him.

I was stupid enough to do it long ago.

Maybe from the moment I first saw him and wanted him to be mine.

CHAPTER FIFTEEN

JOSH

"So, any chance of hanging out this weekend?" Matt asks tentatively.

I smirk and shake my head. I have plans this weekend. I want to take Giselle sailing, but something is up with her, and I don't know what it is.

Scratch that...

I have an idea. I think she wants to know what's happening with us. I'm trying to get my head around it so I can give her my answer. The answer that's in my heart.

Friday is supposed to be our last day together working here, and the last day of us the way we are.

That was the unwritten contract and understanding. Things have changed though.

I got the job and will be managing the new branch of Tanners, but I'm sitting here worried about getting the girl. I want her to be mine completely.

"Any chance of ever seeing you again outside work?" Matt asks, leaning against the table.

We've been meeting up here at the coffeehouse in the mornings and sometimes late like this.

"Of course. Let's plan something," I laugh.

"Plan, like the last time you canceled a sailing trip we planned months in advance?"

I still feel bad about that, but not so much when I think of what I got in return. It was a trip with the guys worth sacrificing. I will never, ever get the image of Giselle in my bed wearing that yellow lingerie set out of my head. She's right—yellow is her color, but then I fucking love her in anything and any kind of color.

I take a sip of my coffee and raise my hands.

"I won't cancel this time. We'll go sailing in a few weeks."

He inclines his head to the side and frowns at me. "Weeks, Josh?"

God, he's the one with the girlfriend, and he still has time for the guys. Me, though, I'm obsessed with my girl, and I can't get enough of her no matter how much she gives. I still can't get enough.

"Let me check my calendar later, and we'll set a date for two weeks." I think that's reasonable.

"Okay... that sounds better. And in two weeks, will you still be under this contract of yours with Giselle? I mean, will you be extending it, promoting her, or ending it?"

I stare at him and rest my elbow on the table. The thing about Matt and me is, we've always been real with each other. He's the guy I tell my secrets and my inner thoughts. He's the guy I trust.

"So... the situation is this. I don't want to extend it, and I don't want to end it."

"You want to promote her?" he asks carefully, and I find myself nodding slowly.

"I just don't know how to go about it. Matt, I'm not boyfriend material. And before you tell me you aren't either, don't. We're different. We just are. I want her to be with somebody who deserves her, and I'm too selfish to let her go. At the same fucking time, I know Dad is going to lose his shit if he sees me with her."

"Does it matter if you have the job?"

"The man's not stupid. That won't matter. She was just the stipulation because I was directly working with her. I know he doesn't want me doing the same shit I used to with anybody, her included, even if we aren't working together anymore."

He narrows his eyes at me. "There's nothing against that here. You're allowed to have relationships, especially if you aren't even working in the same building."

"I know, I just... it's just shit. It brings be back to point one. I don't know how to be that guy she needs. She's been weird with me since yesterday, and I think it's because we haven't talked about what we're going to do."

"Josh, this is bullshit. You don't pussyfoot around shit. Do you want the woman?" he asks.

"Yeah, I want her." But what do I do if she doesn't want me?

That's the question I'm not asking myself because that's never happened. I could be here sitting on my thoughts, thinking the ball's in my court when it might not be. She said she wasn't feeling well last night, so I left her alone. She went home, and it was the first night in weeks that I spent away from her. It was the strangest feeling ever. What if that was just her way of starting the distancing process?

I've never even done that. Giselle would be the first who would hurt me if she didn't want me because I'm the playboy prick who wanted to own her body.

I'm the playboy prick now who wants more than that. I want the rest of her.

Heart, mind, and soul. *Everything*. The missing pieces to what I already have.

"Josh, this is a no-brainer. You know what to do. Tell her how you feel. I think it will be okay if you did. You talk and lay the cards on the table. Then you don't have to worry about it. Take back control, man."

Yeah, he's right. This situation has knocked me off kilter and made me go soft.

I know what I want, and I'm going to make it happen.

She's in my office organizing the files when I get back. The plan tonight was to finish up here and end the night at my place.

She hasn't said anything about that, though, and she's still sporting that cautious expression from earlier.

It's close to seven and nearly everyone has left the building.

She smiles at me when she sees me, and I reach for her, slipping my arm around her tiny waist.

"Josh, we should finish here," she tries to protest. When she looks at me, I see the dimness in her eyes and a slight pink tint, like she's been crying.

"What's wrong with you, baby?" I ask her, and she studies me.

She shakes her head and brushes her fingers over my chest. "It's nothing. Nothing's wrong. I'm still not feeling myself."

I catch her face and lift her chin toward mine so she can look directly at me.

"Baby, do you remember when we first met, and I told you that I watch?"

"Yes... I remember."

"Good girl, so you know I can tell when something's up with you. I knew last night, but I could tell that you wanted to be alone. I can tell now that as much as you want me, you're doing something you've never done before when it comes to me."

"What?"

"Resisting me. You've never done that, baby, and I don't want you to start now that we only have a few days left here, working together."

Now that I don't have the job to worry about, I want to focus on her. I want to focus on her and plan to deal with Dad later. But only if I get the chance I want with her.

"Tell me what's wrong," I prod, and I'm shocked to shit when a tear runs down her cheek.

I wipe it away, but another follows. She gets that one.

"I had a run-in with Riley."

"You what?" Jesus Christ, I've gone from mellow to psychotic in seconds. "What did he say to you?"

"Josh, please... don't get upset. He just pointed out a few things I think I should have been aware of and wasn't."

What the fuck did he say to her?

I'll kill him. Beat him senseless this time so he'll know not to try anything next time.

I take her shoulders. "Tell me what he said," I demand.

She draws in a deep breath and tells me. She tells me what she wants me to know, and because I'm so observant, I know she didn't tell me everything.

By the time she finishes, I'm ready to bring down Armageddon on Riley's ass. Realistically, though... I am ready to end him, but I can't say the man was a liar.

He used the truth against me, and she knows it's the truth.

She's been her usual nice self as we've spoken, never offending me. Not once pointing out the obvious truth.

We met at The Dark Odyssey, and the way I've been with her at the place, it's like I live there. I'm the devil in my nest of sin, cozy, like one of the owners. Like I'm rubbing shoulders with the Giordano pack who own the club. Meaning she'll know she wouldn't have been the first woman to indulge me there. She'll know that night she first met me was because I was on the prowl for a woman to live out my next fantasy with.

She'll know I'm the devil because I've kept telling her I am.

We look at each other as she finishes up. I'm still holding her.

Holding her and thinking now more than ever that an angel like her shouldn't be with a devil like me.

Look at her—she's beautiful. Inside and out.

"He's kind of right, isn't he?" she says. Her voice is meek. I can't answer her. I don't want to confirm it. "Josh, why did you pick me? That night you first saw me. My birthday. Why me? There were so many women you could have gone for. I stood out from a mile away. It was so clear that it was my first time there, that I wouldn't have been used to any of the things we've gotten up to. I'm sure without me saying it, you must have figured out that you're the second man I've ever been with. Why on earth would you want me?"

It's all those things. All of it.

I look at her now and actually understand the obsession, but I feel worse than I already did.

She's unbroken, untainted. Delicate and innocent. She's different.

I like different, and I saw her and only her in the sea of women at the club. I saw her then and wanted her, badly.

Like I want her now.

I can't answer because I don't think she would understand, and I can't begin to explain that she makes me want to be different too. Just the devil when I'm with her.

So, I show her. I lean forward and claim her lips.

I kiss her and pull her close, so close I taste her, taste her everywhere, except I'm still just kissing her lips.

I'm so focused on her that I hear nothing and see nothing else.

It's the time that counts, though, because she must have heard enough for the both of us.

Her eyes go wide, as she looks over my shoulder.

I turn to see Dad.

CHAPTER SIXTEEN

JOSH

Dad is watching us with complete disapproval.

"Just for once, I truly hoped it wasn't true," Dad snarls. He looks from me to Giselle, and I release her. "Just like always, with every woman who works for you, you just couldn't leave well enough alone, could you?"

He walks away, slamming the door, and I look back at her feeling more exposed. His words are a tell of what I am.

Fuck... what the fuck do I do now?

"I should go," Giselle stutters.

"No, wait." I reach for her, but she shakes her head.

"Josh, I... need to be alone."

She leaves too, and I stand there like an idiot. Dad and Giselle leaving me here.

Dad saw us together. What the hell does that mean for me now?

I march down to his office and through the door that's already open.

He's standing by his window, fuming.

He whirls around to face me with rage, more rage than I've ever seen in him.

"What the hell do you expect me to say to you, Joshua?" Dad barks. "I asked you to do one thing, and that was to stay away from her. That was the main thing. When Riley told me you'd been seeing her, I couldn't believe it."

"Dad—"

"What? Are you seriously going to deny it? Tell me he's wrong? I saw you kissing her, and it didn't look like a kiss that just happened. You're involved with her, possibly the whole time."

"Yes," I confess. "I was. But it's not what you think. It's not what any of you think."

"Joshua, women are like toys to you. I'm so disappointed in you for the way you are. It's shameful sometimes to think of you as my son, and I'm supposed to let you represent my company when you can't even keep your dick in your pants?"

The truth is all coming out tonight.

I've just realized something, though. I've had enough. I've had enough of it.

It looks like I may have lost it all, so I may as well shed the remnants of what's left.

"No, you shouldn't. You shouldn't have me represent your company. I shouldn't work for you at all."

His lips part, and shock suffuses his features.

He looks stunned, but I don't know what gets me more—that or the fact that he doesn't stop me when I leave.

———

I stayed awake last night.

Couldn't sleep at all. I went straight home and first sat in the study looking through the window trying to figure out what I'm supposed to do.

I then ventured into the TV room, switched on the TV, and watched the classic films marathon that was going on.

I saw three of the films Giselle likes. *Casablanca, Some Like It Hot* and fucking hell, I brought the morning in with *Gone with The Wind*. It was the only film I watched in color. The rest were in black and white.

She loves them all, and I watched them trying to feel close to her, yet I'm so far away in my mind.

I feel like shit by the time morning truly breaks and I'm sitting in the kitchen eating Cheetos instead of heading for a shower to get ready for work.

Jobless and girlfriend less. That's me.

Jobless for sure. It's what I am after I quit. I'm sure to own the girlfriend-less part means I would have had to have the girlfriend in the first place.

The doorbell rings, but I don't answer it. Juliana has a key, and I'm not expecting her today.

Matt doesn't know what shit happened to me, so I doubt it's him, and I especially doubt it's Giselle. She wouldn't come here by herself.

So, whoever it is can fuck off.

I don't want to see anyone today.

I need to figure out what I'm doing. Not with work. With Giselle.

The shit happened with Dad, but the part I'm stuck on is her. Because... I still want her. I'm just not sure she should be with me.

I hear the front door open and scowl.

The tension recedes from me, however, when Dad walks into the kitchen. I forgot he has a key to my place too, but no way did I expect him to be here. Not when he's so ashamed and disappointed in me.

"What are you doing here, Dad?" I ask.

He sighs and gives me an uneasy look.

"I'm here to talk, son," he answers.

"Dad, I can't. I don't want to. I should think you'd be more relieved than anything to get rid of me. Now Riley can have the job, and you won't have to feel bad to pass him up an opportunity you wanted to give him in the first place."

"That's not true, Joshua," Dad says, shaking his head. "The job was yours from the moment I decided to open the branch. Then you really pissed me off with the temp, and I knew Riley wanted the job too, so I... did what I thought was best."

"Dad... I didn't do anything with anybody to be classed as unprofessional. I get that my previous behavior was shit, but I wouldn't have gone to the new branch and give you a bad name. I wouldn't have planned to do that. But it doesn't matter anymore."

"It does because I want you to run the place, Joshua. Last night, I said something I shouldn't have, and I admit this competition wasn't fair on you. I saw that you changed, but I was taking precautions when I thought you hadn't. I didn't want to lose Giselle the way we lost Marsha, or any of the other women you pissed off. I saw her talent and wanted to keep her. Joshua, I need you for this job. Riley is good, but you're the best."

I look at him and consider it. It's all been too much that I'm not sure how I want to proceed.

"If I take it, I don't want you breathing down my neck. I want you to trust me to have a handle on things. I want you to trust that I got things under control, and mostly, if I have a chance with Giselle, I want you to allow me to see what I might have with her."

He stills and his face softens. "You really do like her?"

"Yes. I do."

He nods. "Okay... I will do all of that. If... if I may, it seemed to me like she might feel the same way about you."

"Well, I don't know. Since you both seem to know what I'm like, I'm not sure what chance I have with her."

"Joshua, I'm here today not because you're my son and I feel like I should give you everything. I'm here today because I know I have something good. Someone good. The best. If she knows that, I guarantee you, you have a chance."

That's perhaps the nicest thing he's ever said about me. "Thank you, Dad... I appreciate that."

He nods. "It's the truth."

Truth. I guess for her to know the truth, I'd have to tell her.

Maybe that's the answer, and nothing else will matter.

Just the parts I want where I showed her how much I wanted to be with her.

CHAPTER SEVENTEEN

GISELLE

"Hey... take it easy on yourself," Rachel says.

She reaches across the table and takes my hand.

We've seemed to gather here at the coffeehouse more than normal since I've been seeing Josh.

I know he's kind of done the same thing with his friends during our very wild whirlwind romance.

It's been wild.

Past tense... I keep pointing that out to myself, and every time I do, my heart aches.

I don't want us to be past tense, but what am I really doing? What the hell am I actually doing thinking I can have more with a guy who just wanted to have fun with me? Sex. It was about sex. Sometimes it wasn't, but it was more often than not.

"I'm trying to separate things out in my mind," I tell her.

As usual, she came to my rescue. We've already consumed the most fattening things in here—a slice of cake for me and a sugar bun for her, then we each had another two slices of cake each. All in the space of an hour.

I'll have to leave soon. We're five minutes away from work,

but I can still be late with the way I'm feeling. Or not turn up. It did cross my mind, but that would be completely stupid. I would be very stupid to do that. I can't lose a job I worked damn hard for because I fell for a guy I shouldn't.

"Giselle, we've been eating, and I've just been here trying to resemble the friend I should be. I know I'm probably not much help, but talk to me," Rachel says.

I feel bad as I look at her. It's clear she's going through stuff with Dante. He's back now officially, and his fiancée right alongside him.

"How about you talk to me? I know you're going through stuff. You've been here for me, and I feel like because of the newness of all I went through with Josh, I needed you more, and I haven't exactly been there to talk to about Dante."

She smiles. "There's nothing really to talk about. It's just me dealing with my feelings for a man I can't have. I felt terrible whenever I've been with them because I can't shake off this thing I've always felt for him. There's nothing more to say than that, and nothing I can do besides forget and move on. So, please, allow me to be here for you." She dips her head and tucks a lock of her hair behind her ear.

"Please promise me you'll talk to me if you need me."

"Yes, I promise. I absolutely promise I will do that. Now, come on, talk. I know the core details. You told me what happened, but those are just details. I know you want to be with Josh. Tell me about that."

"I don't want to get hurt again, Rachel. I don't want to get hurt and broken the way I was when Kirk dumped me." I draw in a sharp breath.

"I think that was obvious. Of course, you don't. But if you allow fear to rule you, you'll never do anything. You'll never be with anybody. It was okay when you and Josh were fun, but even I could see, and I haven't really met him properly, that it stopped being about fun a long time ago."

"But what if it was that only for me? What if it can't be more?"

"You know what? I'm going to allow the only person who can answer that question to do the talking for me," she laughs. "Just for the record, he looks at you the same way he did that first night at the club."

I don't know what she's saying to me. She looks up ahead of us, and then I see him.

Josh.

He's standing over by the door and is looking at me.

I glance back at Rachel, and she nods.

"Go, I'll be fine. Call me later."

"Okay," I answer and rise to my feet.

I make my way over to Josh and stop just before him. We look at each other for a few seconds, then he holds out his hand to take mine.

I give him my hand, and he leads me away.

We go to the park by the lake and sit on the bench.

It's one we've come to a few times. I enjoyed making out with him and watching the scenery. The ducks swimming by and the peacefulness of the place.

We're sitting on the bench together again now, and he hasn't let go of my hand. He's still holding it and looking down at it.

Then he looks up at me with a little smile that pulls at the corners of his mouth, bringing the dimple out in his left cheek.

He pulls my little silver coin from his pocket and holds it out to me.

"My coin." I'm not sure what he means by showing it to me.

"Yes, your coin." I pause as my heart stills. "Are you giving it back to me?" I ask, swallowing hard against the lump that's formed in my throat.

"No, I'm not. It's permission."

"What for?"

"A chance."

"What kind of chance?" I ask.

"I have this fantasy... it's fifty years from now," he declares.

"Fifty years?" I smile. "That's a long time."

"Yeah. It's you and me fifty years from now. We might not be sitting on this bench, but we do this," he says, lifting my hand. "People see us together, and we're that couple who is always holding hands. Our kids can't stand it, but our grandkids are a little different. They think we're the cute old couple. We always sit like this and watch, even if we don't talk. The silence is fine because it's all part of the fantasy. You and me, we're it."

I bite the inside of my lip to keep from crying, but damn it, a tear slides down my cheek. I'm listening to what he's saying and taking in the beautiful vision of something I want too with this man.

"That's us fifty years from now?" I ask, unable to hide the quiver in my voice.

"It is, baby. I can't see it any other way. I look ahead as far as I can in my mind, and all there is, is you. It started when I first met you. I looked at you, and I wanted you, decided I had to have you, and I can't think past that part. Everything else revolves around that." He stops and pulls in a deep breath. "Riley wasn't wrong about me. I won't pretend that I'm a saint, or that any of what he said about me being a playboy isn't true. It was. And that's just the thing—it *was*. You deserve to be with a guy who can love you and love everything there is about you. I do. I love you. I love you, but I won't claim to deserve you. What I want is a chance to. If you can give it to me, I promise not to break you. I promise that all my fantasies will be only shared with you. That's my answer to why I picked you, but also my plea for a chance. I want you and me. I want the chance for that. Can you give it to me?"

I don't have to think. I don't have to contemplate the answer to that question at all. He just told me he loves me. That means everything.

"Yes. I can. It's not just me who is deserving of love, Josh. You are too. I love you, and I want to be the woman in that fantasy fifty years from now."

"You already are, baby. Come here," he says, beckoning me for a kiss we both fall into. It's beautiful and filled with all the wild passion we've shared.

It's the kind that keeps coming. It grows, and it goes higher and higher. It fills my soul, cascading through my being.

It's everything I've ever wanted.

Just like him.

EPILOGUE

GISELLE

Four months later...

It seems fitting that we'd celebrate our engagement in our favorite room at The Dark Odyssey.

The playroom.

I'm chained to the bed with the blindfold over my eyes while Josh is feeding me fruit.

I love how he changes each fantasy up, and I can't wait to see what he has in store for me tonight.

He places a strawberry in my mouth, and I eat it at the same time he sucks the cream that covers my nipples.

Tonight, he's not only chained me to the bed, but he's covered me in cream and fruit. I'm dessert.

This is tonight's fantasy, and I'm loving it.

Everything else can stay outside in the world, away from our bubble of bliss.

We work together now in the new building, away from everyone, and we're a good team there too.

Whether it's work or play, we do it well. I especially enjoy the playing parts.

He continues to feast on me, going lower and lower until he reaches where I crave him most.

"This is a prep for the wedding, Future Mrs. Tanner," Josh says.

"Is that so?"

"Yes, I have it all planned out. I have an hour booked to devour your perfect pussy, and then your sexy-as-fuck ass. Imagine what being married to me will be like, my perfect little sub."

I smile. "Fifty years of fantasy."

"Like fuck. Fifty was just the minimum quota. We're forever, baby," he informs me, and I grin from ear to ear, loving the sound of that.

"Forever sounds great."

"It sure does."

It does. I can't believe this is me.

I did it. I became the confident, sexy, daring woman, and I fell in love.

Thanks so much for reading.
If you enjoyed Giselle and Josh's story, check out Rachel and Dante's story in Tempt.

ACKNOWLEDGMENTS

For my readers.
Always for you.
Thank you for reading my stories.
I hope you continue to enjoy my wild adventures xx

ABOUT THE AUTHOR

Faith Summers is the Dark Contemporary Romance pen name of USA Today Bestselling Author, Khardine Gray.

Warning !! Expect wild romance stories of the scorching hot variety and deliciously dark romance with the kind of alpha male bad boys best reserved for your fantasies.

Be sure to join my Sassy Dolls readers list *for some exciting, mouthwatering, seductive romance xx*

https://www.subscribepage.com/faithsummersreadergroup

Join my reader group -

https://www.facebook.com/groups/462522887995800/

Made in United States
Cleveland, OH
07 January 2025